TRAILS WEST:
WESTERN STORIES

TRAILS WEST

Eugene Cunningham

GUNSMOKE

First published in the US by Five Star

This hardback edition 2013
by AudioGO Ltd
by arrangement with
Golden West Literary Agency

ISBN 978 1 471 32085 9

British Library Cataloguing in Publication Data available.

Printed and bound in Great Britain by
MPG Books Group Limited

ACKNOWLEDGMENTS

"Beginner's Luck" first appeared in *Frontier Stories* (2/27). Copyright © 1927 by Doubleday, Page & Company, Inc. Copyright © renewed 1955 by Eugene Cunningham. Copyright © 2000 by Mary Carolyn Cunningham Call and Jean Cunningham Weakley for restored material.

"The Hermit of Tigerhead Butte" first appeared in *Frontier Stories* (3/27). Copyright © 1927 by Doubleday, Page & Company, Inc. Copyright © renewed 1955 by Eugene Cunningham. Copyright © 2000 by Mary Carolyn Cunningham Call and Jean Cunningham Weakley for restored material.

"Wanted — ?" first appeared in *Frontier Stories* (5/27). Copyright © 1927 by Doubleday, Page & Company, Inc. Copyright © renewed 1955 by Eugene Cunningham. Copyright © 2000 by Mary Carolyn Cunningham Call and Jean Cunningham Weakley for restored material.

"The Hammer Thumb" first appeared in *Frontier Stories* (6/27). Copyright © 1927 by Doubleday, Page & Company, Inc. Copyright © renewed 1955 by Eugene Cunningham. Copyright © 2000 by Mary Carolyn Cunningham Call and Jean Cunningham Weakley for restored material.

"The Trail of a Fool" first appeared in *Frontier Stories* (7/27). Copyright © 1927 by Doubleday, Page & Company, Inc. Copyright © renewed 1955 by Eugene Cunningham. Copyright © 2000 by Mary Carolyn Cunningham Call and Jean Cunningham Weakley for restored material.

"The Ranger Way" first appeared in *Frontier Stories*

TABLE OF CONTENTS

Foreword

by
Murney Cunningham Call

Foreword

by

Murray Cunningham Cull

Born into a proud Texas family, my father grew up with a love of Texas—and her people, past and present—which only intensified as he met and listened to old-timers. As a child, he would run away from home—always to be found around some cowboy campfire he'd joined earlier, soaking up every scrap of their memories of the old times, the land, the people and their histories. He never forgot anything he'd heard, and built on these yarns in the stories and books he wrote as an adult.

Underage, he found someone to pose as his father, giving a birth date that got him into the U.S. Navy, where he eventually served during the Great War. Following active sea duty while the Great War was still being fought, he was sent out as a Navy recruiter. We children found these recruiting recollections far more interesting than naval skirmishes because in El Paso, Texas, he met and recruited our mother, Mary Caroline, as one of the very first naval "Yeomanettes" in the country, forerunner of WAVES today. She was sent from Texas to serve in San Francisco, Eugene Cunningham's home base.

After the war, he accepted a newspaper assignment taking him to Central America. In numerous letters prior to his homecoming in 1921, he persuaded Mother to return to San Francisco to be his bride. He assured us she chased him all the way to the top of City Hall, where he tried but couldn't climb the flagpole, so he married her. For years, we'd stare in awe at pictures of that building and its flagpole. Although I knew better by the time we moved to San Francisco, it continued to fascinate me whenever I passed it.

They settled in San Francisco, and he wrote a book about his Central American adventures, including some with the legendary General Lee Christmas, GYPSYING THROUGH CENTRAL AMERICA (1922). In 1925 my parents returned to El Paso to await the birth of their first child—me. My sister, Jean, and brother, Cleve, were also born there, in 1929 and 1933, respectively. Daddy enjoyed living and breathing Texas—especially in the colorful border town of El Paso, steeped as it was in the excitement of the early days of Texas and the Southwest. He lived and breathed cowboy history; and—blessed with a photographic memory and an insatiable curiosity—he could give detailed answers to any question, on that or any other subject one could bring up. For a brief time in the arrogance of my youth, I checked his answers but gave up after many attempts, finding he was never wrong.

All history, of any era, interested him, but Western and Southwestern history always came first. He loved all things Texan—and Southwestern—and cowboy! My older daughter, Karen, would run to sit, mesmerized, at his feet whenever she saw him put a cigarette in the ashtray. She couldn't believe he would always make a perfect new cigarette, using just one hand. He rolled his own in wheat papers with Bull Durham until the day he died. From earliest childhood, I can remember him singing—or whistling—any of the many old cowboy songs. To this day I treasure his battered and torn old Lomax book of cowboy songs. He knew them all, popular or obscure. I can still hear his rich baritone and the clear, sweet trills of his whistling. Kirsten, my younger daughter, would stop all activity to concentrate on him alone when he'd sing, humming—in a monotone—along with him, repeating the hum whenever he'd pick her up, obviously convinced she was repeating his songs back to him.

As a child, I was privileged to accompany Daddy on some of his shorter trips around Texas and New Mexico, visiting old Texas Rangers or notorious gunmen of the past. It was so exciting to hear him swap yarns and encourage reminiscences that I'd fight to stay awake and not miss a word. Although I didn't fully realize who many of them were, I enjoyed the excitement. Two Texas Rangers in particular, John R. Hughes and James B. Gillette, visited us—and we them—fairly often. Their adventures entertained us above all others, and enhanced our pride in the men who tamed the Wild West. It was also a thrill for me to read the galley proofs of Daddy's books, and recognize, here and there, bits of tales I'd once heard, late into the night.

His circle of friends and acquaintances was catholic. He found everyone interesting: the old gentleman with a shoe shine stand in the lobby of his office building, the "Mexican Dulces Shop" workers down the street, politicians, doctors, lawyers, judges, gunmen—lawmen and outlaws—he enjoyed conversations with them all. I delighted in occasional visits—and was enthralled by letters—from writers like Eugene Manlove Rhodes, Ernie Pyle, J. Frank Dobie, Nunally Johnson, Dashiell Hammett, Roarke Bradford, Albert Payson Terhune, and Erle Stanley Gardner, among others. Visits usually included a trip to Juárez for a bullfight, though not for us children. We could tag along when it was only dinner across the border, where we awaited outcries about the rich, spicy foods from his Eastern guests. When Daddy returned from infrequent New York City trips, he'd regale us with colorful bits about sitting in at the Algonquin with the coterie of writers there whom he knew, especially about those he admired. He was a great judge of character. Notable among friends I remember, probably because he kept the autographed pictures they sent him on the walls of his scriptorium and because I'd seen their faces in the movies—or at least heard of them—were William S. Hart, who wrote congratulatory letters after reading each of Daddy's books, Tom Mix, and Ken Maynard. There were other, later, movie cowboy heroes, including John Payne, who credited his books with providing insight into the minds and habits—and gunslinging talents—of early gunfighters, but these earlier ones were my favorites. Memory fades when I try to picture others.

He had so many yarns dancing in his head, demanding to be put on paper, that he needed to use a multitude of different pen names. Often many of his stories filled, sometimes to capacity, an issue of one or another of the Western magazines. I wonder how many readers, seeing different authors listed, had an inkling they all came from the same scarred fingers on an early electrified typewriter he designed after his fingertips were accidentally cut off. He wrote frequently as Leigh Carder, and, when he wrote a novel set during the Great War, his publisher insisted he was too well known as a Western historian and novelist to use his own name, so they published DEEP SOUNDINGS (1937) under the *nom de plume* of Alan Corby. *Time* magazine had quite a spread at the time on the "mystery" of the book's famous Western author.

Daddy was an absolute perfectionist about his writing, and an impeccable wordsmith, turning memories and legends of earlier years into stories and articles and books. There is a constant ring of truth to all his tales, since he wrote for the joy of writing—and of sharing old-timers' accounts of history as they had lived it, as well as history as he had lived it.

Even more in life than in his writing, his droll sense of humor frequently sneaked up to clobber one, unaware! Many a friend of mine would—hours later—gasp and ask: "Did I

really hear your father say . . . ?" Karen affectionately remem-
bers now—but at the age of five didn't see through the adroit
question—"Do you want to see the rattles from my rattlesnake?"—whenever he decided it was time for her to leave
him in peace. This was delivered with an innocent smile, but
with a devil in his eye. Before he could reach for the desk
drawer where he kept his rattlesnake, she would high-tail it
out of there, posthaste! Another favorite display of humor occurred whenever he was standing on the Sutro Heights bal-
cony, out of sight, admiring our view of the ocean out to the
Farallone Islands. If tourists—or anyone—passed by, wondering aloud over something, his deep voice would boom out,
god-like, with the answer they sought. No one ever saw him,
and many times—"My God!"—rang out in various tones of
exclamation or questioning.

In the early civilian days in El Paso, he worked in an adver-
tising agency, writing for himself in his free time. Later
writing jobs were sandwiched in between his own writing, included being Literary Editor for El Paso *Times* as well as
doing book reviews and articles for *The New Mexico Magazine*
for several years. An omnivorous reader, two of his favorite
authors were women: Dorothy L. Sayers—whom he'd often
quote to us—especially her Peter Wimsey mysteries; and
Mary Johnston, who wrote about "days when knighthood was
in flower." (His single bit of chauvinism reared its head when
he praised them for "writing like men." He always encour-
aged Jean and me to try anything we wanted, then to do it
well.) Westerns were the only genre he mostly tried to steer
clear of reading, wanting to keep his writing from any chance,
however inadvertent, of being colored by information he
himself hadn't gotten "from the horse's mouth" or from
someone standing near the "horse."

It tickled him when a nephew wrote he was basking in reflected glory among his fellow soldiers because TRIGGER-NOMETRY (1934), his book on gunfighters, was being used by the Army to teach about guns and fast draws for special units during the Second World War. Yet, his interests in life were as broad as his circle of friends. He always managed to find some thought-provoking nugget hidden in everything. He learned to work with his hands from his father—a master cabinetmaker who also built one of the first roller coasters in Texas—and there was nothing in the way of furniture he couldn't craft, or mechanics he couldn't master. We still have tables I can remember watching him make in his leisure hours. It was one of these tables, I might add, that cost him the fingertips of one hand when—as a curious young child—I bumped into something in his workshop, and the noise shattered his concentration. Because of that accident, and the tenderness of those fingertips, he designed a plan to electrify his old manual typewriter, to make it work with a softer, gentler touch from those scarred fingers. I can't think of anything we wanted that he couldn't make or improve.

While waiting for our Sutro Heights home to be built overlooking the ocean, Daddy rented a nearby home to oversee the progress. The first time Jean saw that house—on a steep San Francisco hill—she burst into tears, sobbing that all our furniture would slide down the slanted floor and break. He calmed her by promising to replace any furniture that broke.

Hours spent tramping through old cemeteries, reading faded inscriptions on aged tombstones (many of those interesting names and quotes found their way into his writing), filled me with his enthusiasm for that fascinating pastime that I, in turn, passed on to my daughters as a living legacy from their beloved "Dandear."

His dedications—long or short—were precious to all of us. In BUCKAROO (1933), when he wrote my dedication—

"For Mary Carolyn, who didn't get to ride in the rodeo parade that time, this book is affectionately dedicated, as a poor substitute for that ride she missed, by its and her author," Jean complained: "You're always doing something for her! You never decorate a book to me!" He complied by writing, in DIAMOND RIVER MAN (1934)—"To Jean this book is 'decorated' "—and it took many corrections of corrections, plus compromise quotes around the disputed word, before proof readers at Houghton Mifflin realized he was insistent that it read "decorated!"

A few years after our move to San Francisco, remembering his talented and inquiring mind, his former captain requested his return to the Navy for special assignment in an Intelligence unit. He accepted the commission. He could see war clouds looming and kept insisting Japanese war lords would eventually attack Pearl Harbor and then the Philippines. Frustrated by the lack of positive response, this time he and the Navy bitterly parted company. After the Pearl Harbor attack, to play a part in the war he worked in the Richmond shipyards. Mother also did her patriotic bit, working her way up to second-in-charge of a classified government war effort. We had a victory garden of vegetables (including his favorite, artichokes), but kept a small part of the back yard flower garden, so Daddy could continue to grow the sweet peas and the baby roses he remembered from his mother's gardens. Over the years, his dental health had deteriorated, due mainly to neglect during his cowboy days. After years of trying to fight the pain by drinking, he celebrated the end of the war and his own personal victory by finally seeking dental care and then eschewing the now superfluous drinking. The change in him was dramatic! He began writing again, after a long dry spell. First came articles and short stories, and eventually two new novels—although only one, RIDING GUN

(1957), was completed and published before he died, back in the saddle, at the top of his form.

Eugene Cunningham wrote a total of fifteen stories about the adventures of Stephen Ware, Texas Ranger. They appeared with some regularity in 1927 and 1928 in *Frontier Stories*, a monthly magazine then published by Doubleday, Page & Company. In the late 1940s many, but not all, of these stories were reprinted in *Zane Grey's Western Magazine*, published by Dell Publishing Company, and for a second time enjoyed great success among readers. Nine of these stories have now been collected for the first time in book form in TRAILS WEST.

Beginner's Luck

The gang pounded south through the Crazies by way of Dead Man's Gap, pushing the stolen Swayn Thoroughbreds hard down the cañon. Black Alec Rawles rode point. The Kid, in the rear, kept the band from breaking back toward home, while Charro Joe and the Chink, covering the flanks, watched both the horses and Myra Swayn, who rode among them with hands lashed to the saddle horn.

When a side cañon loomed ahead, Black Alec whooped to the flank riders, and they loped ahead to cover it, while the Kid pushed the lean, black Thoroughbreds on. All but the Kid knew this wild border country intimately. He had been picked up down on the desert after the raid, a shambling, overall-clad, seventeen-year-old vagrant of a cowhand. Black Alec had thought another rider would be useful in shepherding Old Man Swayn's beloved horses across the river to Mendoza's "revolutionary" camp. So they gave the silent, incurious-seeming boy a wiry buckskin to replace his decrepit mount, and he went to work as for wages with no show of any emotion upon his brown face.

He had not seen Old Man Swayn hammered senseless to the earth of his dooryard by Black Alec's loaded quirt butt; the two Triangle Bar 'punchers shot dead in the bunkhouse door by the Chink and Charro Joe; or Myra Swayn roped to a horse while the famous Thoroughbred herd—that Mendoza, nicknamed "The Broom," so coveted—was gathered. But the curt talk of the Chink and Charro Joe told him as much of

21

that as he could have known had he been with them from their start south of the river. What he thought of it all, the others never inquired, nor did his smooth face tell anything of his thoughts. He asked no questions about the gang's destination, expressed no curiosity of any sort regarding his profit from the venture.

Toward four in the evening, Black Alec suddenly wheeled his horse and blocked the cañon. The band stopped, milling nervously. In its van the great black stallion watched the man. It was the stallion's fame that had caused the raid, for word of him had gone up and down the Crazy Mountains country, out upon the yellow deserts, across the river to where Mendoza headquartered while he blew up trains, raided ranches on both sides of the river, and thumbed his nose at *Federales*' clumsy, futile efforts to capture him. Two thousand *pesos* Mendoza had offered for the stallion, one thousand *pesos* for any animal from Old Man Swayn's beloved herd.

The Kid whooped shrilly in the band's rear, and the black stallion swerved down the narrow, tortuous side cañon, his harem and the two colts following. Black Alec waited for his followers, a gaunt, slouching figure, black-bearded to his snaky, opaque eyes.

"Them damn' rangers is easy twenty miles behind, I 'low," he grunted to Charro Joe and the Chink. "Hadn't been fer you-all lettin' that Mex kid git away at the ranch, they wouldn't have knowed nothin' about us till we had the hosses over the river an' got the money from Mendoza. Cap'n Reno's hell, too! But the Mex kid had ten mile to ride, an' the rangers had ten mile to come back. They don't know nothin' about this here side cañon, neither. Me 'n' old Enriquez was the only ones knowed he had a cabin in it. We'll smooth up a little here, an' they'll go hellin' on by to take that short-cut fork to the river. We'll rest up at the cabin, an' then, 'bout three in the mawnin', we'll sa'nter out an' head west a piece. We'll hit the river ten, fifteen mile from whar they'll likely be a-waitin' fer us. Charro, you take this old shoe an' ramble on down the main cañon couple mile. Drop it in the trail like as if the stallion cast it, see? Then come on back an' smooth things up around here. Good thing, the cañon's got a rock bottom! They can't tell if fifty hosses . . . or none 'tall . . . is ahead of 'em."

"¡Sta bueno!" nodded Charro Joe. His weasel-face twisted in a sinister, one-sided grin. "I'm fix them shoe so them damn' ranger, she's think she's *see* them stallion drop him!"

He spurred off, riding as only a Mexican can. Black Alec, with the stolid Chink and the Kid trailing, followed the band to where, six or seven miles from its beginning, the side cañon ended in a grassy park of perhaps two acres. It was a blind cañon. The tiny spring, the grass, made it ideal for their purpose, but it had the disadvantage that from end to end of it the high, sheer walls were unscalable even by a man afoot.

Myra Swayn's mount had halted with the other animals near the little, half-ruined stone cabin. The Chink swung down and unsaddled; the others followed suit. Black Alec went over to the girl and stood for a moment staring up evilly into her white, set face, for which the widened, fearful blue eyes seemed all too large. She was only sixteen or so. Suddenly Black Alec grinned and loosed the rope that shackled her ankles together beneath the horse's belly, that which held her wrists tight to the saddle horn.

She toppled sideways into his arms, and he carried her up to the cabin. When he halted to set her down, he laid his bearded face in a bear-like caress against hers. When she jerked against his arms and made little despairing noises in her throat, the Kid saw his shambling body shake with silent laughter. The Kid watched with his habitual lack of expression. The Chink's blank yellow face was unaltered, but into his slanting, lashless eyes leaped a sudden reddish light.

While the Chink fried bacon and made coffee and the Kid brought more firewood, Charro Joe rode back and unsaddled. He threw his hull down against the cabin wall and started to take the Winchester from the saddle scabbard, but the girl moved slightly—Black Alec had tied her hands and feet again—and he left the carbine to come and stare down at her. Black Alec squatted in the cabin doorway, smoking. He paid no attention to the Mexican. But the Kid, sitting upon his ancient, battered saddle halfway across the cañon, saw Charro Joe's hands suddenly tremble and clench hard, saw how he lifted his head a little to eye Black Alec furtively. Then he moved on and sat staring broodingly at the ground.

They ate in complete silence. Black Alec loosed the girl's hands and set a piece of wrapping paper before her on the ground with a meager meal of fried bacon, cold black beans, and leathery tortillas upon it. Charro Joe and the Chink watched him, eyed each other sidelong, seemed to come to some mutually satisfactory understanding, and again turned their eyes toward Black Alec.

"*¡Por Dios!*" cried Charro Joe suddenly, with his sinister, one-sided grin. "She's one good time, *sí*. Seven *caballos* an' them damned stallion. Mendoza, she's pay us nine thousan' *pesos,* an' them Ol' Man, she's have three thousan' dollar in *la casa*. Fifteen thousan' *peso* . . . for Black Alec, for them Chink, for Charro Joe. Ho! An' las' year, this time, me, I'm dig them rock in them chain gang at El Paso."

Neither Black Alec nor the Chink made any reply. But Charro Joe had a definite purpose in talking—as the Chink's lidless, smoldering eyes seemed to see. He leaned back

24

against the cabin wall and rolled a cornshuck cigarette of inky tobacco, lit it, and inhaled an enormous cloud of smoke. His slender right hand was upon his knee; he lifted his head a little, and laughed thinly.

"Fifteen thousan' *peso*. But, *por Dios!* I'm forget them girl! How we're divide one girl for three?"

"Don't you be worryin' about that," Black Alec drawled ominously. "The girl . . . she's mine."

"So-o?" Charro Joe's eyes flashed to the Chink, then sinisterly to Black Alec. "So-o? Now, me . . . an' them Chink . . . we're think she don't go like that. Ever'thing w'at we got, she'd divide for three."

Suddenly the hand upon his knee held a knife—held it delicately by the point. The Chink's hand, also, had been armed with legerdemain as flashing. Either of them could impale a cigarette paper at twenty feet, as Black Alec knew from observation. So he sat motionless. His hands were close to Colt butts; men along the border called him amazingly fast on the draw, a marksman with either hand. But now those knives would be hurled into his throat while his fingers curled about Colt butts. Kill them both, he could—he felt sure of that—but it would be while dying. He was equally sure of that. He decided to temporize.

"I brung her along. You-all never would've done it," he grumbled. "But if you want to start a row about her, here's what I'll do . . . two thousand *pesos* of my share fer her. You-all can split it a thousand apiece. If that ain't fair. . . ."

"Not five thousan' *peso!*" cried Charro Joe. "No, *amigo!* Me, I'm not take five thousan'."

Slowly, but with infinite emphasis, the Chink nodded agreement with this.

"Well, then, s'pose we-all plays poker for her?"

"Play poker weeth Black Alec?" The Chink spoke for the

first time, and his scornful question was full reply.

"We shoot them craps!" cried Charro Joe. "Me, I'm got them dice."

"*No sabe* craps." Now the Chink eyed Charro Joe suspiciously.

"W'y, she's ver' simple. Mos' luck. *Por Dios,* Chink. S'pose you never play him, you're mebbe have them beginner's luck."

He spread a Navajo saddle blanket on the earthen floor of the cabin, near the fire. The twilight was fading. The Chink threw more wood on the fire, and red, flickering glares dappled the red-and-gray Navajo blanket. Charro Joe produced a pair of cheap, red celluloid dice and rolled them across the blanket.

"Ho! Come 'long them seven!" he cried.

"Hell! Might's well make it interestin'," grunted Black Alec. "Let's figure the girl's worth three thousand *pesos* . . . thousand apiece. That'll make each share six thousand *pesos*. Each one of us'll take sixty matches, each match bein' a hundred-*peso* chip. We'll shoot fer the whole works. But we'll shoot fer the girl, first. Mebbe the feller that wins her'll want to put her up ag'in."

They nodded assent, Charro Joe with one-sided grin, the Chink suspiciously. They explained to the Chink the rules of the great game of craps. They would peewee for possession of the dice for first roll, ace high, low shoot. Charro Joe demonstrated the peewee roll with the dice, and the Chink nodded. Then there came the dull, expressionless voice of the Kid from behind the tense, watchful trio.

"Where do I come in on this, misters?" he asked. "Mebbe I got some of this beginner's luck a-comin'. I never shot craps."

They whirled upon him, startled by his noiseless approach, by his unusual display of interest, his altogether odd departure from the dull taciturnity they had come to expect from him.

"God damn!" snarled the Chink ferociously. "I'm cuttem heart out."

But Black Alec caught his wrist. With left hand he held the knife hand motionless, while his own right hand flicked up. The heavy quirt that hung on his wrist—the quirt that had pounded Old Man Swayn down and down in his dooryard—leaped up like a rattler's length to wrap clear around the Kid's head. He staggered, but was upheld by the tension Black Alec kept upon the quirt lash. When it was jerked free, the Kid reeled backward with an inch-wide crimson welt upon his face.

He was unarmed. Nothing more than a barehanded attack could be expected from him. Yet Black Alec, even while he swung the quirt to and fro, kept left hand at gun butt, as if doubtful whether to kill or quirt him, if he moved. But the Kid only raised his hand to his welted face.

" 'Scuse me, misters," he mumbled.

"Listen. You git back an' herd them hosses. Let 'em feed up an' down. If one of 'em looks like he wanted to break downcañon, I'll turn you over to the Chink here. He'll cut your damn' heart out an' show it to you! Watch that damn' girl, too. If she starts anything, call me *pronto!*"

The Kid backed off into the darkness. They stood staring after him, the Chink still malevolently snarling of face, Charro Joe grinning his sinister, one-sided grin. From the darkness came an odd, gasping sound. It was not repeated.

Charro Joe's grin climbed a little. "*¡Por Dios!* He's cry! W'at the hell!" he jeered.

From rim to floor the cañon was now filled with almost

palpable darkness. Far, incredibly far above a myriad stars, softly yellow, luminous as topazes, spangled the blue-black sky dome. Ten feet away, the cabin doorway became a vignetted, ruddy glow that seemed to hang in the dull-white expanse of wall. The shape of it altered from moment to moment as the firelight flickered or the men inside moved. The girl—motionless as if dead—was but a log-like bulk along the outside of the wall.

"Ho!" came Charro Joe's thin voice from the cabin. "Them Chink, she's have them beginner's luck, *sí!* She's get them dice. Now, Chink, you're roll them dice an' pray for them natural. But, first, you're put up w'at you're want to shoot. Three hundred *peso,* w'at? *Bueno.* Me, I'm make two hundred, an' Black Alec, she's cover one hundred."

The girl shuddered. She had heard all the details of the gambling arrangement. She was struggling silently but furiously against the pliant rawhide that pinioned her wrists together and shackled them to the loops about her ankles. Suddenly she felt eyes regarding her. She turned awkwardly, to stare up with dilated eyes. The flickering light from the door shone upon one side of the Kid's face as he looked down upon her. It turned his bronzed face into copper, made it seem hard, inhumanly set, like a statue's. She found no hope of aid there.

The Kid moved off as noiselessly as he had come. Presently the horses moved a little. The girl saw their black shapes and heard the muffled snorting as they grazed. From the cabin Charro Joe's voice sounded again. This time the Mexican's laugh held little of mirth.

"*¡Por Dios!* One more natural! Them beginner's luck, she's look . . . not . . . so . . . much . . . like . . . them . . . beginner's. . . ."

"Cover him, Charro," grunted Black Alec. "I'm goin' to

take a look at them hosses."

He appeared in the doorway, to stand staring across the cañon at the horse band. Something moved in the darkness at the girl's feet. She sensed, rather than saw or heard, it. Black Alec's animal-keen ears caught some tiny, rasping sound. He whirled, automatically half drawing his Colts, falling into the cat-like crouch of the gunman.

"Kid?" he snarled. "Kid? Whar you? Damn your soul, I'll. . . ."

A moment of silence, then from the horse band across the cañon came the Kid's flat voice.

"Yes, sir, mister. I'm watchin' the hosses."

Black Alec grunted. He shoved the guns back into their holsters and came past the girl. She shrank away against the wall, but he went on and fumbled with his saddle. When he came back, he halted in the light of the door, teeth glinting in the tangle of black beard. Upon his palm were two red cubes. He held them in his cupped hand, close to his ear, rattling them. All the while he grinned.

"Beginner's luck," he said softly. "Beginner's luck. Well . . . mebbe."

He went inside.

Charro Joe was cursing steadily now in a spitting, cat-like monotone. *"¡Por amor de Dios!"* he spat out a triumphant oath. "She's time! Me, I'm lose eight hundred *peso* to them damn' Chink! Give to me them dice!"

So noiselessly, so abruptly that she almost screamed, breath was upon the girl's cheek.

"Gal, will you go along with me?" a voice was whispering in her ear. "You got to do what I say now."

A knife blade touched her wrists, and the rawhide fell away, touched her ankles, and she was free. Roughly he chafed her wrists. She sat up and tried to stare at him, but the darkness was a curtain between them. Inside sounded the thud of the dice upon the Navajo blanket and Charro Joe's steady cursing. She shivered at thought of those three villainous faces, intent upon the roll of the dice that would finally tell whose property she became. Sudden panic possessed her—panic that made this other one here seem almost a protector, seem a desirable alternative.

Flashingly she tried to recall more of the detail of him. He had been only a slender, dust-coated shape during the day, glimpsed at intervals when despairingly she turned to see if rescue showed on the back trail. Not much to build a picture on, but of the four she preferred to go with him, since go she must. She rose and caught at his arm. He let her cling to it as they moved toward where the horses pawed and snorted.

The horses moved a little at their approach—all but two. The Kid pulled free of her, then stooped to loose the picket ropes that held these. Apparently, she thought, he had counted upon her willingness to go with him, rather than remain with that gang. Or perhaps he had intended to carry her off anyway. They were thirty, forty yards from the door now. He gave her a foot up into a saddle and himself flashed upon his mount without touching stirrups. Suddenly the firelight was blocked by a man's figure.

"Hey, Kid!" Charro Joe called. "W'ere you are?"

"Here, mister! Just watchin' the hosses!"

The girl heard again, beside her, that odd, gasping sound the Kid had made as he had moved off after taking Black Alec's quirt across his face. This time she recognized it as laughter.

" 'Sta bueno," nodded Charro Joe. Then he turned easily toward where the girl had lain. "Them girl! Black Alec! Chink!" he shrilled.

He ran a few steps in the direction of the silent pair. He

had jerked his gun now. He leaned forward to stare this way and that. A rifle exploded almost in the girl's ear. She shut her eyes instinctively and opened them to see Charro Joe running desperately toward the cabin door.

"You missed him!" she cried angrily, then was furious at the partisan-interest that had leaped up in her for this strange figure beside her.

"Not with a rifle," he answered calmly. "Come on. Here's where we high-tail it."

A shrill yell, and the horse band broke down the cañon. A rifle bullet dancing upon the rocks at their heels and they were stampeded. Behind them, Myra Swayn and the Kid rode hell-for-leather in a burst of shots from the cabin.

At the mouth of the side cañon the band of Thorough-breds whirled north—back toward the Triangle Bar. With a sudden, wild impulse Myra Swayn set spurs to her animal and followed. But of all the band the Kid had chosen to ride the great, black stallion. Even in the darkness the girl knew that tall bulk. A hand caught her bridle reins, and both horses slid to a halt. So that chance was gone, she thought, almost resignedly—*if* it had been a chance. Fifteen miles south was the river.

"Don't you be in such a hurry, gal. I got a little talkin' to do," the Kid said.

But then he was silent for perhaps two minutes. She waited, with odd mixture of emotions, of which curiosity was dominant.

"Those hosses, of course, will break right for home. Only . . . they'll meet rangers. Maybe that'll scare 'em and send 'em back this way. Hmm. Well, can't help it. Listen, now! You'll pour the quirt into that *caballo*. You'll meet Captain Reno an' the rangers. You'll tell the captain that Ware's Kid's squattin' up here, ridin' herd on what's left of Black Alec's San Simone

31

gang. They've got five, six miles to walk, and they can't get out except here . . . walls too steep. An' they won't get out here!"

"You . . . you aren't going to take me to Mexico?"

"Hell, no!" he cried earnestly. "What'd I want with you? Only thing I want is to get in the rangers. That's what I came along with Black Alec for . . . what I've been working for all the time. There's two vacancies now, but Captain Reno told me, the other day, there's five hundred after those jobs. Asked me . . . dern his hide! . . . who'd I ever fight? And him and my pa was rangers together!"

He whirled the black stallion and turned back toward the cañon mouth. The girl stared blankly after him, then spurred on.

She was three or four miles up the main cañon with the horses closed in upon her when a hand seized her wrist, and she began shouting for Captain Reno. Reno answered in amazement, recognizing her voice. She poured out her story in a torrent of words, but the ranger grasped the urgent portion after a moment, and she was swept around and back toward the waiting Kid, still talking.

They raced on, but long before they could reach the side cañon a spatter of shots reverberated from the rocky walls. Reno swore viciously and spurred on recklessly. Another burst of shots, then scattered, methodical-seeming shots, finally ominous silence.

"Here it is!" cried the girl, recognizing the mouth of the side cañon.

The rangers drew rein quickly. As they sat their horses, staring tensely at the black mouth of the cañon, something moved beside a boulder. The shape was covered by four guns in a twinkling.

"Captain Reno," a flat, toneless voice called weakly. "This is the Kid. I . . . you came too . . . late. They came a-bustin' . . . to get out. . . ."

The dim shape crumpled, and Reno was off his horse to catch the Kid. He lifted the slight figure from the ground.

"Black Alec and . . . the Chink . . . came a-bustin'. I had to kill 'em. The Chink . . . he . . . carved me up a little. Nothing much. Does this . . . you reckon . . . does this . . . get me into the Texas Rangers?"

Eagerly, forgetting his "carved" shoulder, Ware's Kid tried to look up into the captain's twisted face.

"Son," said Reno ferociously, "she shore as hell do!"

The Hermit of Tigerhead Butte

Upon the flat mesa Alamito seemed to sleep in the brilliant sunshine, a sprawling huddle of gray-brown adobes against the green forest of the Bajadas, beginning here behind Alamito in the tumbled foothills.

Ware's Kid let his big black stallion choose his own way in and out among the houses, along the zigzagging, dusty byways that served the town as streets. His brown, expressionless face, enshadowed by the huge brim of his Mexican sombrero, seemed to point always straight ahead. But the level, gray-green eyes saw without seeming to see—a trick of Stephen Ware that had disconcerted quite a few of his acquaintances—saw everything before and to right and left of him.

The stallion passed the squat church with its stubby twin towers, passed the ragged, green plaza before the church, came to the line of stores and saloons that faced the plaza. Here the deserted aspect of the town was explained, for upon the deep adobe-pillared verandah were gathered the men of Alamito, talking earnestly.

Ware's Kid drew rein at the hitch rack before one of the stores. He sat the stallion for a moment, staring expressionlessly at the Alamito folk on the verandah. In turn, they stared quite curiously at him—a smallish figure, eighteen or nineteen at the most, sitting the tall stallion as if horse and rider were of one piece, like a carven chessman. His great Mexican sombrero was of black felt, its band and edging of silver lace. He wore a waist-length jumper of soft, tanned goatskin, the sleeves fringed to the elbow with a huge bunch of flowers embroidered in vividly colored silk upon the back. His *pantalones* were of fine blue woolen cloth, slashed in Mexican fashion along the outer seam and belling at the bottoms over his boot toes with rows of silver buttons on either side of the scarlet insert in the seam. On his high heels were enormous Mexican spurs, ornamented with hammered silver and with tiny bells hanging on the shanks.

These details of his costume they noted, as they observed the sweet little Winchester carbine, caliber .44, in the hand-carved scabbard beneath his left leg and the long-barreled, white-handled Colt that hung—too high for any gunman's fancy—upon his right thigh.

He swung down, nodded to them, threw the split reins of his Mexican bridle over the hitch rack, and twisted them deftly into a looped half-hitch, then came at the stiff-legged gait of the cowboy-born onto the verandah, to pass through the wide doorway into the dim, cool interior of the store. There was a lean, hawk-faced man at the far end of the rough counter, talking earnestly to a tense group. He eyed Ware's Kid flashingly, then nodded.

"Durham. Papers. Matches. Crackers an' cheese," grunted Ware.

He squatted in a corner, made a cigarette, then spread crackers and cheese out before him. The thin-faced store-keeper went back to his conversation. Ware's Kid ate and puffed alternately, with inscrutable eyes upon the floor. To him came quite clearly the tall storekeeper's talk.

"Now, what I say is . . . mebbe he killed 'im an' mebbe he never, but if Tom Renault never killed 'im, then . . . who did? That's whut I say! Ain't he admit that he clumb up Tigerhead Butte las' night? Ain't he admit that he owed Starke fifteen hund'd dollars? Ain't he admit that it couldn't been more'n a hour after he left Starke's cabin . . . after payin' the fifteen hund'd, he says . . . before Starke was killed . . . us seein' the fire like we did when the cabin burnt right at nine o'clock? Shore he did!

"An' who else'd want to kill Starke? He never had no trouble with nobody in this country. Mebbe he did keep to hisself, like, livin' up there on Tigerhead Butte with just that big dawg an' that Mexican boy an' not talkin' much when he come to town. But is that there reason for anybody killin' him? That's whut I say! No, sir! It shore looks to me like Tom Renault, he's elected!"

Ware's Kid was interested, but only vaguely so. He was in Alamito on a very definite errand and more than a little proud that, out of all the force, the adjutant general should have summoned him, little more than a year a ranger, to Austin, and should have given him this independent detail of tracking down Dell Spreen.

Alamito's murders, however interesting in their details, were no concern of his. So he curbed his natural, professional curiosity and got up slowly. He slapped the cracker crumbs from his clothing, nodded slightly to the storekeeper, and went outside, boot heels clicking upon the rough-planked floor.

The townsmen on the verandah were also discussing the murder of this Starke, the hermit of Tigerhead Butte. Ware's Kid stood motionless for a moment, until a lithe, overalled youth turned presently in his direction.

"Marshal around?" inquired Ware.

"Office," replied the cowboy, with equal terseness. He jerked a thumb vaguely. "One up. One right. One left. Sign."

Ware's Kid nodded thanks and loosed the stallion's reins. He swung up and turned in the direction the cowboy had indicated, made the right turn and the left, and saw, before him, midway down a row of adobes, a crudely lettered legend on a dingy board—**Marshal**. He dismounted and again tied the stallion. There was quite a crowd before the marshal's office. It was with difficulty that Ware's Kid made his way inside.

He identified the peace officer swiftly, a lean, sallow, nervous man with a big, nickeled star upon his tattered, buttonless vest, booted and spurred and wearing two pearl-handled guns in tied-down holsters. At this moment the marshal's roving, brilliant black eyes discovered the stranger. He moved over to Ware.

"Yeh?" he inquired with a shade of truculence in his voice.

"Marshal?" grunted Ware's Kid, noting, without betraying it, the suggestion of bullying in the peace officer's bearing. "Want to talk . . . to ourselves."

"Say!" cried the marshal. "I'm too damn busy to be a-botherin' with kids today. Idee! Comin' 'round, worryin' me!"

"Wouldn't say that," drawled Ware's Kid. Something electric leaped into the gray-green eyes—a hard glint that, apparently, dazzled the marshal.

"Oh, a'right! Come along outside."

He led the way through the doorway, elbowing through the crowd, and halted halfway down the line of adobes. He expressed irritation, impatience in every nervous line of him, as he leaned against the wall, jammed his hat a trifle farther over one eye, and began to make a cigarette, staring hard at Ware's Kid.

"Looking for a fella," Ware stated briefly. "Figure he come to Alamito from El Paso. Want to find him. Name's Dell Spreen."

"Dell Spreen!" repeated the marshal. He pulled absently

at his mustache. "Dell Spreen. *Hmm!* Uh . . . how come yuh're huntin' Spreen?"

"Want to find him. Has he been here?"

"Whut yuh want with him?"

Again that electric something flashed through the usual dullness of Ware's eyes.

"I want him," he snapped. "I'm going to get him . . . dead or alive."

"Are yuh a Texas Ranger?" gasped the marshal. "Hell. Why, I figgered yuh was just some kid."

"Ranger," nodded Ware's Kid impatiently. "Sent after Spreen. I asked you . . . has he been here?"

"Yes. Left . . . oh, week ago. Headin' for the Canadian, I reckon. But, son, if I was in yore boots, I'd not look too hard for Dell Spreen. Yuh might find him."

Ware's stomach shook convulsively. "I'm Bill Ware's kid," he answered, as if that were answer enough."

"Ware's Kid?" cried the marshal. "That got Black Alec Rawles an' the Chink an' Charro Joe? The hell."

"Who's this?" asked Ware abruptly.

Around the corner of the adobe, something less than ten feet from where they stood, a slim, dark-eyed, dark-haired, amazingly pretty girl had come almost soundlessly. Her eyes were upon Ware, to the exclusion of the marshal.

"Dora Renault," shrugged the marshal. He did not seem pleased at the pleasant sight of her.

"I was coming to ask you if I could see Dad"—the girl turned, as with a real effort, to face the marshal for a moment—"and I heard *him* say he was a ranger . . . was Ware's Kid. I . . . I. . . ." She whirled back upon Ware, with small brown hands outflung pitifully, yet with a certain art in the gesture, a certain calculation in her face. Evidently she knew the effect of her pleading upon the average man. "My father is accused of murdering Lafe Starke . . . a man who lived up yonder on that big butte, five miles from here. He didn't do it. But they . . . the town . . . are finding all sorts of proof that my father must have murdered Starke to keep from paying him fifteen hundred dollars. They . . . they talk of hanging my father without a trial. You're a Texas Ranger. You're Ware's Kid. We've heard about you here in Alamito. Won't you help me? Won't you clear my father? You can! You know you can!"

"Sorry, lady," mumbled Ware uncomfortably. "The marshal here . . . he'll do what's necessary. Me? . . . I got to be going. Got to high-tail it for the Canadian. Orders. Adjutant general's orders."

He tried to move past her at the end of this long speech, but she clung to the fringed sleeve of his jumper. She was crying aloud now, and the sight of her wet cheeks bothered Ware enormously. He was tempted to jerk loose and make a run for his stallion, but she hung to him with strong young fingers. The marshal grinned at his predicament, and Ware's Kid snapped resignedly: "All right! No job of mine. But I'll look around."

"Oh, if you will!" she cried. Magically her tears ceased. "You'll clear him. He rode up Tigerhead last night, Mister Ware, to pay back fifteen hundred dollars he'd borrowed from Lafe Starke. He found Starke in his cabin up there . . . there's a high stockade around it, for the Indians have attacked it several times . . . and paid the money. He got his note and Starke let him out the big gate.

"An hour later, just before Dad got back to town, the people here saw a big fire on Tigerhead. When they got up there . . . meeting Dad and taking him with them . . . the stockade door had been battered down . . . the cabin was burned, and in it . . . in its ashes . . . they found Starke's skull with a bullet hole in it. It was the Indians. He had beaten them off a half dozen times. Everybody knows that. He used to kill two or three in every attack. He'd find 'em sneaking around the woods up there and kill 'em. He was better in the woods than most Indians. They killed him. Killed his big mastiff, too."

"What d'you think?" Ware asked the marshal.

"Well," replied the officer cautiously, "there's some as holds with Dora here. But more says Renault done it for the money. Starke'd been shot from behind."

"Let's take a look. Have you got time to come? No crowd, now, just us two."

"And me!" cried the girl. "I'm going. I'll meet you on the trail."

Ware's Kid and the marshal managed to get out of Alamito unobserved. Dora Renault, mounted on a stocky cow pony, joined them a half mile up the steep trail to Tigerhead Butte, which thrust out like a crouching animal from the slopes of the towering Bajadas. The marshal developed a turn for conversation.

"Queer hairpin, this Lafe Starke," he said to Ware. "Been here nine, ten years. Talked like down South . . . Georgia or Alabama. Never said whar he hailed from. Hunted a lot. Raised wonderful garden truck an' sold it down in Alamito. Rafts of money in that. Used to bore holes in logs an' stick gold pieces in 'em. One time the creek flooded him out. His biggest log floated off, an' he was nigh crazy for two weeks till he found it. Hated Injuns like pizen. When he'd kill 'em, he'd chop off their heads an' stick 'em onto the top o' his stockade. I seen a dozen heads a-seasonin' up there onct. Man! Starke, he was chain lightnin' on the draw."

"Could he hit anything when he'd drew?"

"Oh, I reckon he was a good shot."

"Not much trail," commented Ware's Kid, glancing down at the narrow path they were following.

"Reckon not," the marshal grunted. "That dawg o' his made this section right onhealthy. Never knowed when he'd come out o' the bushes an' have yuh by the throat. Starke an' the Mex boy that worked for him was the only ones that dawg'd stand for."

"He might have been a great painter," the girl volunteered. "He could make three or four lines . . . just like a flash, he made them . . . and you saw a picture. I have a drawing of his at home. It's a wolf jumping at a steer. Just a dozen lines made with a burned stick on a tanned sheepskin . . . but you can almost see them breathe."

"Shore could draw pictures." The marshal nodded. "Just come nat'ral to him, I reckon. Same's talkin' with most folks. He'd be tellin' yuh about a bear or lion he see coming to town. An' he'd grab anything as was handy an' make a few lines an' . . . there'd be what he was talkin' about. I seen him do it in the dirt with his finger. Well, here she is."

They turned an elbow in the steep mountain trail, and there was a twelve-foot stockade built of upright, peeled logs with pointed ends. There was a big gate in its center, hung upon huge wrought-iron hinges. Now it sagged drunkenly. It had been hacked as with heavy axes until even the heavy timbers of which it was made were chopped almost in two. Ware's Kid glanced at it curiously, then his eyes wandered to the mummified heads of Indians with which the stockade top was crowned. The girl looked, then turned hastily away, shuddering.

"He was a hard man, Mister Ware. No wonder the Indians hated him. He killed Cuchillo Colorado . . . Bloody Knife . . . one of the Kickapoos' biggest sub-chiefs, last spring. He made sleeve fringe of Bloody Knife's scalp."

Inside, a heap of gray wood ashes, still smoking faintly, marked the site of the hermit's cabin. Halfway between stockade gate and the cabin lay the carcass of a huge black dog, a fearsome creature. The big head had been battered to a pulp. Ware's Kid thought flashingly that he could remember many badmen whom he would have preferred meeting to that great brute. He swung down and went at his stiff-legged walk about the place.

It was a complete destruction. Nothing left but ashes. To one side had been laid the charred and mutilated skull found in the ruin. It did not require the marshal's significantly pointing forefinger to show Ware's Kid how the townsfolk had deduced that Starke had been shot from behind. There was a small hole in the back of the skull, while the forehead had been blown almost away.

"Well," grinned the marshal sarcastically, after Ware's Kid had poked around for a while, "see somethin' none o' the rest of us could find?"

"Do you know what you found? See tracks?"

"Nah! Too dark las' night. Then it rained toward mornin'."

"Going to take a look outside the stockade. You-all wait here."

He circled the stockade, watching ground and undergrowth. But, as the marshal had said, the rain had washed the soft earth smooth. He widened his circle without result. But when he widened it for the third time, he came out into a little circular opening in the low trees upon a shoulder. The cabin site was visible from here, and Ware's Kid could see the marshal talking to Dora Renault. Then, without moving, he began again his methodical study of the ground. Suddenly he squatted.

In the dry, protected dust were marks made apparently with a forefinger for pencil—a crude, yet perfectly legible, sketch: a cave mouth with before it three pine trees, of which the center one leaned across, almost touching its neighbor on the right. Ware's Kid studied this sketch, obviously the work of Starke the hermit with customary inscrutability. He looked up at the scrub oaks that shielded this little patch of earth.

"Never rained in here," he mused, then rose.

For minutes he had been hearing the sough of running water, and now he found the tiny creek that curved to run downhill past a corner of the stockade. From the place where he had found the sketch to the creek were the matted trunks of small saplings. No sign of a footprint was here. Sight of the creek reminded him suddenly of the hermit's alleged store of gold pieces, hidden in augerholes in logs. He went back downhill to the stockade. The marshal and Dora Renault stared at him, the first curiously, the other hopefully. But his brown face told nothing of the tumbled thoughts behind it.

"Those gold pieces in the logs?" he wondered. "Have you seen 'em?"

The marshal shrugged. "Reckon ever' man that come up here poked for 'em," he said with a dry grin. "Either they was stole an' the logs pitched into the fire, or else they was in the cabin an' got burnt up . . . *quién sabe?*"

"Reckon you're right," nodded Ware's Kid. *"¿Quién sabe?"*

He squatted down, and the gray-green eyes roved over the faintly smoking ashes, over all the minutæ of the stockade's interior. His was a deliberate, but intensely logical, mind and just now he revolved a question. But he had not been impressed over favorably with the marshal, and, just as he had not taken that official into his confidence about the charge of robbery and murder against Dell Spreen, he gave no word now to indicate his suspicions.

"Any strangers in Alamito lately?" he asked slowly, after moments of silence.

"One," nodded the marshal. "But . . ."—his sallow face twisted in a sardonic grin—"I reckon yuh won't hang this onto him. Yuh see, he happens to be a big feller up in Georgia. Hung onto his land after the war an' made money. Now he's goin' to buy ranches for him an' some friends o' his. He never knew they was such a gunny as Starke. Never seen Starke. He was with me . . . Judge Aiken was . . . all o' day before yeste'day an' Starke, he was into town just for an hour or so. Yuh got to do lot better'n that, son."

"You don't reckon this judge, then, had anything to do with . . . this?"

" 'Bout as much as the gov'nor o' Texas."

"Let's go," suggested Ware's Kid, coming to his feet.

"You . . . you've found something?" the girl asked anxiously, spurring up beside the big stallion.

"Marshal reckons not," he murmured, looking down at her from his perch on the tall black. "Hilly country, isn't it? Lots of caves, I reckon."

"Yes," she nodded listlessly. "A few are known, but not many come up here to explore. Starke's dog saw to that."

"Son"—the marshal, who led the way, turned in the saddle to grin unpleasantly at the ranger—"yuh shore yuh're Bill Ware's Kid? I was just a-wonderin' whilst yuh was doin' all that investigatin' back yonder. Waitin' for yuh to ast a kind o' important question . . . what become of Starke's Mex boy?"

"Right. I never said anything about him. You know where he is?"

"I shore do! Now, me, when I go out investigatin' a thing like this, I ast myself who-all could've done it? I looked for

47

that Mex boy. Never figgered he killed Starke . . . Starke was chain lightnin' on the draw. But I wanted to know what become o' him. Happens 'twas me as found a half dozen ribs o' his in the ashes. Yuh want to remember the Mex boys, son."

He spurred forward again, with shoulders shaking. The girl seemed impressed by the marshal's treatment of Ware's Kid. She rode around the stallion, and so Ware's Kid brought up the rear. He seemed heedless of her desertion and rode with expressionless face shuttling from right to left as he watched the country.

They were moving along a narrow bridle path through thick scrub timber, so dense that the foliage almost made a tunnel of the trail in places. Abruptly the timber ended ahead. Ware's Kid checked the stallion on the beginning of a wider track that led downhill and skirted the base of an outjutting shoulder of the mountain. He looked upward to the left, canting his head to stare at the greenery that crowned the mountain shoulder. Suddenly he slipped from the saddle, the little Winchester carbine coming from its scabbard like a live thing.

The marshal and Dora Renault had vanished around a curve in the trail beyond. Ware's Kid turned aside from the trail and, covered from view in a moment by the brush, started uphill, making fair time despite his high heels and moving with a soundlessness that told of no little woods experience. He could not see, for a while, the three pines—of which the center one leaned across, almost touching its neighbor on the right—that were his goal.

At last he reached the summit and crouched, with Winchester pushed forward, in a clump of bushes. Before him was a grassy open, perhaps fifty yards wide. In the bushes that fringed it Ware's Kid saw something move. He waited, and a man crawled out and stood erect, glancing about flashingly.

He waited until the man was a third of the way across the clearing, heading, apparently, for the cave mouth behind the three pines on Ware's left. Then he rose and stepped into the open.

"Howdy, Starke!" Ware's Kid called. "How's everything back in Georgia?"

He was a big man, Starke, with a hairy barrel chest that stretched the calico shirt he wore. He had a long-barreled Colt hung slantingly forward of his right hip. Instead of the usual cowboy boots of that country, he wore moccasins. Ware's Kid, standing with Winchester half lifted, meeting the hermit's cold blue eyes, had a sudden impulse to drive a .44 slug through that set, cruel face. But he checked himself.

Only for a split second was Starke taken aback. Then, before the carbine had moved another inch upward, his hand flashed to his Colt butt. With a flick of the wrist the muzzle was trained upon the small figure of the ranger. The Colt roared twice, the reports so close together as Starke flipped back the big hammer that they seemed almost one.

That sudden light flashed in Ware's Kid's gray-green eyes. His brown face was like that of a statue—a figure expressing fierce eagerness for battle. Starke was even faster with his gun than the marshal's "chain lightning" had led him to expect. Still, the conviction upon which he had risked his life was correct. Swiftly, yet with a certain deliberation, the carbine came up. He was ignoring Starke and what he did, gambling that those flashing hip shots could not be overly accurate. At shorter range, they might have written period to the duel, but both missed by inches, and Ware's heavy bullet, aimed as at a target, drove through Starke's shoulder and knocked him down.

"That'll do!" cried Ware's Kid grimly. "Next one's center!"

He crossed the space between and kicked the Colt out of reach. Then he stood staring down at the hermit's set face.

"You low-down skunk! Threw an old Indian head in the fire, huh? Fixed it so a man gets stretched for murdering you. Then . . . you . . . you *chucho!* . . . then you beat your own dog to death. I hope they burn you alive back in Georgia."

When the marshal and Dora Renault forced their animals through the bushes to the summit, they found Ware's Kid standing over his prisoner. One glance at the marshal's face assured Ware that the officer knew nothing of the hermit's trick. The marshal gaped as at a ghost, coming across the clearing with an expression of sheer disbelief. The girl, too, looked like one in the presence of a specter. She stopped feet away, with a hand at her throat, her dark eyes widened, her face like paper for whiteness.

"Lafe Starke!" cried the marshal. "Then yuh wasn't killed?"

The prisoner glared at him malevolently, as if he were to blame for the situation, then turned his back upon them. The girl seemed suddenly to understand what this meant. She darted across to Ware's Kid and caught his fringed sleeve. She stood disturbingly near to him, and Ware moved uneasily, hunching his shoulder and trying to avoid the tear-wet eyes.

"You did clear Dad," she whispered. "I knew you would." Suddenly, at sight of his restless movements, she smiled to herself. Too many times had she observed the effect of her hand upon the arm of a cowboy not to interpret Ware's Kid's uneasiness as shyness before a pretty girl. "I . . . I'm not thanking you . . . yet," she breathed. "I can't . . . with them here."

"How come yuh found him?" demanded the marshal.

"How come yuh shot at him? How come yuh tuh throwin' down on him? He ain't done nothin'?"

"No-o?" drawled Ware's Kid. "The dirty coyote. He set fire to his own cabin. He beat that dog of his to death. He heaved an old Indian head into the fire . . . after he'd shot a hole through it. Then he and his Mex squatted in the brush and watched you-all mill around the cabin. He told the kid to come up here and wait for him. Drew a little picture on the ground . . . a picture of that cave yonder with the three trees. He was scared. He'd seen Judge Aiken in Alamito, and he lit out. For he knew what the judge'd do, if he saw him . . . he'd tell you-all that Lafe Starke was wanted back in Georgia . . . by another name. He figured to make it look like he was sure dead, just in case anybody ever traced him down here. He figured maybe Renault'd get stretched for murdering him . . . and that was funny. I'm going to take him down and ask that judge if he wants him."

"How'd yuh find out all this?" gasped the marshal.

"By not asking questions about Mex boys! Hell! I knew where that Mex boy was as soon as I saw that picture. And soon as I saw it, I knew there hadn't been any murder. I remembered all those Indian heads on the stockade, and I knew how the trick was done. I reckoned Starke must have had a good reason for doing all that, and I knew if he hated Renault enough to do it just to get Renault stretched, the gal here would know it."

He stopped abruptly, as if wearied by all this talk, more than he would normally say in a week. He motioned for the marshal to keep guard upon Starke and turned toward the cave mouth. Pausing at one side of it, he glanced about him, found a small cottonwood log. This he tossed into the cave so that it stuck upon the floor just inside the entrance. Instantly a shot boomed in the recessed cavern. Ware's Kid darted inside and emerged, a moment later, hauling a spitting, fighting Mexican boy of twelve or thirteen, who still clung to his old-fashioned single-shot rifle, trying to brain his captor with its barrel.

"The money's inside with Starke's outfit," Ware told the marshal. "You can go get it, if you want."

The marshal led the way down the trail toward Alamito, with the Mexican boy behind him, hands lashed to the tieties. Next came Dora Renault on her stocky pony, then Starke and Ware's Kid on the black stallion, the wounded man in the saddle, Ware behind it. Passing a clump of bushes, where a curve in the trail hid them from those ahead, Starke lowered his head and peered stealthily from beneath his arm at the hands of his guard. Something round and hard pressed significantly against his kidneys.

"It's a Derringer Forty-One," remarked Ware's Kid conversationally. "I reckon the judge'll be just as lief to see you dead, so suit yourself."

As they entered Alamito, from verandahs and byways men, women, and children appeared like ants from a disturbed hill. The marshal's bearing took on an unusual erectness, a sort of conquering-hero-returning air. He barely nodded to those who shouted questions, gaping at Lafe Starke, the hermit of Tigerhead. As the little cavalcade drew rein before the door of the marshal's office, a portly six-footer, in frock coat and old-fashioned wing collar and cravat filled the doorway.

"There y'are!" he greeted the marshal in a booming bass. "I have been waitin', suh, fo' the betteh paht o' two hours. I'm considerhin'. . . ." With sight of the prisoner he stopped short. His heavy face turned slowly red. He took one long step forward and raised a hand that trembled, the forefinger stabbing accusingly out at Starke. "Ran Stowe!" he cried. "Afteh ten yeahs!" He reached beneath his frock coat and produced a pocket pistol.

Ware's Kid had slipped to the ground. Somehow, despite the seeming awkwardness of his stiff-legged cowboy gait, he managed to move with the swiftness of a shadow between his prisoner and the infuriated Georgian. His stubby, heavy caliber Derringer covered Judge Aiken.

"I reckon he needs killing, but I haven't turned him over yet. Put down your gun."

Slowly Judge Aiken lowered the pocket pistol. "Y' have the advantage, young suh. But that . . . that thing . . . he waylaid an' mu'dehed my brotheh, who prosecuted him fo' theft."

"He'll go back to Georgia, Judge," promised the marshal officiously. "Yes, sir! Yuh can hang him then!"

"He's all yours," said Ware's Kid, turning away.

When he had elbowed through the crowd, which had eyes only for the group before the office door, a pony's shadow fell across him and a small hand touched his shoulder.

"You . . . you aren't leaving already?" whispered Dora Renault, with her little head askew.

"I . . . yeah, I reckon I'll be headin' out for the Canadian, ma'am. Nothin' for me to do here." He studied his boot toes for a moment. "I'll get my stallion and be high-tailin' it," he said then, without raising his head. "I . . . would you ride a piece with me, ma'am?"

A little understanding smile curved the girl's lips. Slowly, she nodded.

"All right, then," he said hastily. "Outside town. East side. Ten minutes."

She found him waiting beyond the last adobe house of

Alamito. He whirled the stallion, and for perhaps a hundred yards they rode side by side silently. The little, inward smile faintly curved the girl's mouth. Ware's Kid's brown face was expressionless. He was amazingly shy, she decided. She must help him.

"You . . . wanted to say something to me?" she prompted.

"Yeah. Ever see a fella named Spreen? Dell Spreen?"

"Why . . . why, yes. He was here a week, living with his brother-in-law. He left for East Texas three days ago. But. . . ."

"Brother-in-law?"

"Yes. The marshal. But I thought. . . ."

"I knew he was lying!" spat Ware's Kid. "Gone a week. Heading for the Canadian. I ought to kill him!" Into the far depths of the gray-green eyes crept something like an amused twinkle, as Ware's Kid looked down at the pretty, puzzled face. "Ma'am, you wanted to thank me. Well, you've done better. You've helped me. Only one in town I could trust. Only one that mightn't lie. As for . . . anything else . . . I'm a Texas Ranger. Got a li'l lady already. Here!" He half pulled the sleek Winchester carbine from its scabbard, patted it lovingly. "Ma'am, she's the only gal for me. *Adiós*. 'Luck!"

And he was gone with a sweep of broad sombrero, as the great stallion surged forward under the spur—gone toward East Texas on the trail of Dell Spreen.

Wanted—?

Ware's Kid jogged into Dallas, coming from Austin pursuant to special orders of the adjutant general that covered the proposed capture or burial of one Dell Spreen, who was charged with murder and robbery down El Paso way. Horsemen passed him, farmers in wagons with their families about them. All gave the smallish figure on the black stallion a more than usually curious glance. He was dressed like a Mexican dandy—a huge black sombrero, heavy with silver bullion, shading a lean brown face and sun-narrowed gray-green eyes; a waist-length jumper of soft tanned goatskin, fringed from shoulder to elbow and with a bouquet of scarlet roses embroidered upon the back; *pantalones* of blue, with rows of twinkling silver buttons on each side of the crimson insert in the outer seam. Some of those who passed him would have instantly recognized his name. For he had wiped out Black Alec Rawles's gang two years before and so had marked his entry into the Texas Rangers. The tale was a classic over a wide land. But the crowd passed him unwittingly, for his white-handled Colt hung awkwardly high upon his belt, and the canny readiness of sleek, brown Winchester stock to his hand was not readily apparent. Too, he was obviously no more than eighteen or nineteen years old.

On the main street Ware's Kid pulled up, this time to stare broodingly up the shallow cañon of brick and wooden buildings, almost as if he expected to see Dell Spreen—a small, deadly figure of smooth, fierce brown face and murderous black eyes—take a step from a doorway.

A drowsy idler upon a saloon porch, leaning comfortably against a post with feet in the dust of the street, promised information. Ware's Kid spurred over, and at sound of the stallion's hoofs the lank one opened his eyes lazily.

"Sheriff's office?" inquired Ware's Kid politely.

"Git to hell out of here an' find out, if you-all's so cur'us!" snarled the loafer.

"Sheriff's office?" repeated Ware's Kid.

Finding icy greenish eyes boring into his face, eyes lit by an uncanny electric sparkling, the loafer sat suddenly stiff-backed. " 'Scuse *me!*" he cried shakily. "But I . . . I shore thought you-all was a greaser. Yore clothes an' yore . . . yore. . . ."

Ware's Kid ignored the profuse flow of apologies. Having received his directions, he rode on. The lounger mopped damp brow with a sleeve and peered after the tall black and its small rider.

"Gawd! He's a mean 'n', I bet you!" he said. "Gent what packs a six-shooter, but reaches fer his carbine when he's riled . . . I bet you he's a wolf."

Ware's Kid swung down before the sheriff's office and hitched the stallion to a splintered post. With carbine cuddled in his arm, he crossed to stand in the doorway of the office. His roving eyes made out, in the duskiest corner, a small figure squatting against the wall.

Ware's Kid went inside. The squatting one was a boy of fifteen, barefooted, in faded overalls, gingham shirt, and ragged hat upon tawny hair. His round eyes were of the palest blue, and he had neither brows nor lashes, so that his gaze seemed unwinking, like a snake's.

"Sheriff?" asked Ware.

The boy jerked his head toward the street door and shrugged silently. Ware's Kid, after a long stare, lounged over to another corner and himself squatted upon his heels.

Presently, he forgot the boy in the opposite corner. Slowly he produced Durham and brown papers and methodically built a cigarette. This he laid upon the floor before him and rolled another, then a third, fourth, fifth, sixth. They laid in a neat row. He picked up one from the end of the row and lit it.

He wondered if he were really to find Dell Spreen here in Dallas. He had not been in Carwell with Sergeant Ames, on the day three months past, when Simeon Rutter and two O-Bar riders had spurred into the tiny, sleepy village with the word of the murder and robbery of Eph Carson, Rutter's partner. But the sour-faced ranger sergeant had told him of the crime and of his investigation at El Castillo, the long, low rock wall from behind which Eph Carson had been shot.

Piecing together the testimony of Rutter and the 'punchers and adding the result of his own observation, Ames had made a fairly complete story. Carson had been on his way back to the O-Bar with about seven thousand dollars of his and Rutter's money. During his absence, up Crow Point way, this gunman Spreen had ridden up to the O-Bar and asked for Carson. Told that he was absent, Spreen had said grimly that he would wait. But shortly after breakfast on the day of the murder, while the ranch house was deserted except for the Mexican cook, Spreen had disappeared. None had since seen him. Spreen knew that Carson was to return with a large sum of money. The whole ranch had known it.

Evidently, said Ames, Spreen had ridden up the Crow Point trail to ambush himself where it ran along the rock wall in the desert—El Castillo. He had not waited long—there were but two cigarette stubs in the trampled sand. Eph Carson had come squarely into range of the steadied rifle. Then two shots, and the wizened little cowman had side-slipped from the saddle to sprawl face downward, dead.

Having robbed the body, Spreen had vanished as if the ground had swallowed him.

Ware's Kid went over the details of his own investigation. He had located the niche in the wall that had held the murderer's .44 rifle. He had re-created the murder, had interviewed Rutter and the O-Bar boys. The dark, bitter-tongued rancher had told how he had ridden with the 'punchers up the trail toward Crow Point, when Carson's failure to return had alarmed him, told how they had found Carson sprawled upon the sand, found his horse a quarter of a mile away with bridle reins caught in the ocotillos.

Two weeks after the murder a peremptory summons had come to Ware's Kid from headquarters in Austin. He had found the adjutant general determined to stamp out the wave of crime then sweeping the border country. He wanted this Spreen killed or taken. Preferably the latter, that he might be hanged upon the scene of his crime.

"You wiped out Black Alec's gang," the adjutant general had said to Ware's Kid. "So I'm giving you this commission . . . get Dell Spreen! I don't care where you have to go to get him, either."

Ware's Kid, who was now smoking the fifth cigarette from his lay-out, was aroused from his thoughts by footsteps. A stocky man clumped inside the office and sat down at the battered desk.

" 'Mawnin'," nodded the stocky man. The rigidity of his angular face was broken up by curiosity, as wide, alert brown eyes roved over the Mexican finery. "Somethin'?"

"Don't know," shrugged Ware's Kid.

He noted that the man wore a deputy sheriff's badge upon his open vest. He was, perhaps, twenty-nine or thirty, although dark mustache and tiny goatee made him seem older. He was dusty as from long riding. Now he reached down stiffly and took off his spurs.

"Don't know," repeated Ware's Kid. "Sheriff?"

"Sheriff's up to Austin, a-powwowin' with the gov'nor. Art Willeke . . . Art's chief dep'ty . . . he's ramblin' 'round the ellum-bottoms, Denton way, huntin' Sam Bass."

Mention of the notorious outlaw, who was just then keeping rangers and peace officers frantic, solved a part of Ware's puzzle. He had been wondering whether or not to take the local officers into his confidence, tell them frankly whom he sought. He decided to forego any help these easterners could give in locating Spreen—an East Texas man and, perhaps, one known to them—to gain the greater advantage of working without danger of warning being passed to Spreen by some friend.

"Kind of interested in Bass," he told the deputy thoughtfully. "Ranger. Headquarters Troop. Name's Ware."

"Ware?" cried the deputy, staring hard and somewhat unbelievingly. "Heerd about you-all. Glad to meet you."

He shook hands and sat down again, still eyeing Ware's Kid doubtfully. Then the boy in the corner came silently to the desk. The deputy nodded to him, hesitated, and turned back to Ware's Kid. "Mind if I talk to him, private?" he asked apologetically.

Ware went outside to lean against the wall. He could hear the boy's excited whispering, an occasional explosive grunt from the deputy. Then he was called inside. The boy was gone.

The deputy sat scowling down at the desk, *tap-tapping* the curving black butt of the long-barreled Colt at his hip. He glanced up at Ware's Kid with the odd, appraising stare he had given the small figure at first mention of his name. "My name's Bos Johnson," he remarked abruptly. "You-all make yo'se'f to home, here. I'll be back right soon."

He was gone fifteen or twenty minutes, and, when he came in again, his face wore that expression of grim rigidity that Ware's Kid had marked upon him when first he had come into the office.

"All right," he grunted. "Le's git yo' hoss to the stable. Then I'll buy you-all a drink."

They saw to the stallion's stabling, then crossed the street to a low, brick saloon. There were not many in it—a cowboy or two, a knot of farmers standing together far down the bar. But, drinking alone, was a huge man with sullen red face and close-set black eyes. He turned at the pair's entrance, staring.

"Whiskey," said Bos Johnson tonelessly. Ware's Kid nodded agreement.

The big man watched, tugging at long mustaches and snorting loudly as if at his private thoughts. He watched belligerently while the bartender poured the drinks for Ware's Kid and Bos Johnson.

"Bartender!" he bellowed suddenly, and crashed a huge fist upon the polished bar.

"Yes, sir?" replied the bartender. His pasty face was gray-hued. "Yes, sir."

"You-all know who I am, bartender? I ask you-all . . . don' you-all know what I am, huh?"

"Yes, sir, Mister Branch. 'Course, I do. Everybody knows Bull Branch. Shore do."

Bull Branch continued to glare menacingly at him. "Bartender," he growled, "since when is Mexicans 'lowed to come a-shovin' in yere a-drinkin' with white men? You-all git down there an' take that 'ere drink away from that Mex. Then you-all chase him outten here 'fore I git mad."

Slowly the bartender inched toward Ware's Kid—who had not yet seemed even to glance in Bull Branch's direction.

When he was still six feet away, the ranger turned his head a trifle—and regarded the bartender. The unhappy man stopped instantly, shrinking back before the uncanny electric sparkling in the gray-green eyes. Slowly, then, Ware's Kid wheeled to face Bull Branch.

"Where *I* come from," said the ranger in a soft drawl, "every gent kills his own snakes."

"What?" roared Bull Branch, lowering big head on bull neck and glaring ferociously. "*Whut?*"

"Pop your whip, fella," Ware's Kid invited him, still in the bored drawl.

Bull Branch gaped amazedly. Deliberately he pushed back his coat flaps and put huge hands upon his hips. The pearl-gripped butts of two Colts showed, almost under his fingers. Then he bore slowly down upon the ranger, who stood sideways to the bar, with left elbow resting on its edge. Bos Johnson moved unobtrusively away from the bar and out of possible line of fire. But Bull Branch made no move to draw his guns, merely came on ponderously.

What followed was blurred like the action of a rattler's head as it strikes. The left hand of Ware's Kid moved—so rapidly that none there actually saw it move. It caught up the whiskey glass from the bar and flipped the stinging liquor squarely into Bull Branch's face. As the huge figure reeled, hands going to tortured eyes, Ware's Kid shot forward. He twitched Branch's Colts from their holsters and hurled them into a corner. He rained blows upon Bull Branch's face—leaping clear off the floor to reach that height.

It was cat and mastiff. Blindly, Bull Branch tried to push him off, but those hard fists, landing with force terrifically out of proportion to the small body behind them, cut his face to ribbons, closed his eyes to puffy-lidded slits, drove sickeningly into his mid-section. He staggered about the barroom, grunting, whining, helpless. At last some instinct seemed to show him the door. He broke for it at a staggering run, and Ware's Kid, with a Comanche yell, leaped upon his back and spurred him through it, catching hold of the lintel and swinging down to the floor as Bull Branch lurched through and fell sprawling upon the verandah floor outside.

When he came back, the bartender was half crouched against the back-bar with eyes bulging. Bos Johnson and the other patrons were clinging to the bar, some whooping feebly, others too weak to do more than shed happy tears. Bos Johnson waggled a hand at the bartender.

"Set 'em up, bartender," he gasped. "This 'n's on the house. Ware! Mebbe they won't neveh hi'st no monument to you-all here, but Bull Branch . . . he'll remembeh you-all plenty."

Back in the sheriff's office, Johnson turned suddenly serious again. He sat staring at the wall. His harsh face rigid as if set in bronze.

"I got you-all into that trouble with Bull Branch," Johnson said suddenly. "Done it a-purpose."

Ware's Kid merely waited, brown face, gray-green eyes revealing nothing of his thoughts.

"Wondered if you-all really was Ware an', if you was, how much o' the talk was so. Because . . . I shore do need some help."

"For what?"

"To go out with me tonight an' stand up to Sam Bass's gang."

Ware's Kid studied the grimly earnest face. From the beginning he had sensed something unusual about him. He thought that Johnson was usually a happy-go-lucky cowpuncher and a man efficient with either hands or weapons.

He was used to judging men quickly, and he began to like this stocky deputy.

"All right," he said curtly.

"You-all willin'?" cried Johnson. "Then here's the lay-out. They're goin' to stick up the eastbound T and P ag'in at Eagle Ford. Figger folks won't be expectin' lightnin' to hit twict in the same place. Me 'n' you . . . we'll be in the weeds 'long the track."

"How come just us two?"

"I could raise a posse," Johnson admitted. "But . . . how'm I goin' to know the fellas I line up ain't in with Bass? No! I'm goin' to line my sights on Simp Dunbar an', before I let some damn' spy carry word, I'll go it by myse'f."

"Simp Dunbar? Who's he?"

"He's the skunk that killed my cousin Billy. Two weeks ago, oveh in Tarrant. Man, I'd give a black-land farm to git me Simp Dunbar oveh my front sight. An' I shore will. 'Twas like this. Bass's outfit loped up to a saloon on the aidge of Fort Worth, where Billy, he was havin' a drink. They was some kind o' wranglin', Billy bein' the kind as won't back down fer no man livin'. Simp Dunbar . . . I've knowed him all my life fer a useless cuss, an' Billy knowed him, too . . . he shot from off to one side. Billy an' me, we helled around togetheh when we was kids. Punched cows togetheh, out Menard way. I . . . I thought a heap o' Billy. . . ."

Ware's Kid nodded silently. Here was a man he understood. Understood his vindictiveness, for it was in his own fierce Texan blood, understood his willingness to take a hundred-to-one chance to face his enemy. More and more, he liked Bos Johnson. "All right. We'll hunt 'em up," he agreed. "How come you know they're going to be at Eagle Ford?"

"My spy told me. Had him a-watchin' fer 'em last two weeks. That boy."

Ware's Kid stared silently at Johnson.

"What's name that other little station . . . east of here?" Johnson asked.

"Didn't even know there was one," shrugged Ware's Kid, with a ghost of a grin. "Johnson, we'll be at Mesquite, not Eagle Ford, tonight. Boy's lying. In with Bass, likely. Feeling I got, and mostly my feelings are right."

Johnson was won over to acceptance of the altered plan, if but half willingly. He admitted that he knew nothing much of the boy, who had appeared in the office a month before offering to spy upon the Bass gang.

"In with Bass," repeated the ranger. "Hell! He could've brought you lots of news before this."

They waited until nearly dark, then ate at a Chinese restaurant. It was pitch dark when they went swiftly to the stable where Johnson's horse, with the big stallion, had been fed an hour before. They saddled, talking a little for the benefit of any ears that might be stretched toward them, of the western road, that toward Eagle Ford.

For a couple of miles they rode swiftly eastward, then turned south on the road to Mesquite. They were close to the railroad always, riding through woodland. Johnson led, because of his knowledge of the country. Soon he checked his mount and jerked the Winchester from its scabbard. Ware's Kid already cuddled his carbine in the crook of his arm. They rode on again, slower now.

Suddenly, not fifty yards ahead, a man scratched a match. Gently Ware kneed the stallion around, feeling, rather than seeing, that Johnson was doing likewise. There was no alarm while they moved back a hundred yards and slipped off their animals.

"Let's hitch the hosses an' sneak up," whispered Johnson.

They returned to the point from which they had seen the flare of that match, the stocky deputy making no more sound than a shadow—than the ranger himself. Then they halted, squatting on their heels, to listen. There was the sound of men moving, of horses, the hum of low-voiced, jerky conversation.

"Late again!" a boyish voice complained. "Hell! You'd think we were passengers, Sam, way the damn' railroad's treating us."

"Don't ye fret, Bub," a harsh voice answered the youngster. "She'll be a-ramblin' along right soon. Ingineer, he'll see that log, an' he'll jerk her back onto her tail right sudden."

"Ever'body lined up?" inquired a pleasant voice—Bass's, Ware surmised. "Yuh-all know where yuh work?"

As the voices answered in affirmative grunts, the ranger began moving soundlessly to circle them to get nearer to the point where the train would stop. Johnson followed until they were squatting in a little open perhaps fifty feet from the track, sheltered by a fallen tree.

"You-all was shore right," breathed Johnson. "Wouldn't be nowheres else in the world."

Minutes ticked off, then there was the sound of the train, far away. The rails before them began to hum. The train was upon robbers and officers with a roar. Came a frantic squealing of brakes and the scream of the whistle.

The train had barely halted when there was a rattle of shots along the track. It was so dark that there was no clue to the robbers' positions save the orange flames that stab-stabbed the night. Ware's Kid was conscious that Johnson was gone from beside him. He wasted no time thinking of that, but ran crouched over up to the track, where he could fire at the robbers' shot flashes. From here he went into action with coldly precise fire from the carbine.

"Who's that damn' jughead?" someone roared. Evidently, thought Ware's Kid, he was believed to be some misguided member of the gang, firing into his own people.

From between the cars came shots to answer the gang now. It was pandemonium, there in the pitchy night, with the heavy roar of Colts and the sharp, whip-like reports of rifles. A man could but guess, by the relative positions of the flashes, at whom he shot.

The ranger hardly expected to do much execution—his position made that a matter of chance. But he was worrying the Bass men.

Suddenly a high, clear voice rang out, crying a name over and over again, penetrating even the staccato din of the firing. "Simp Dunbar! Where you-all? Simp Dunbar . . . ?"

A voice answered, but there was no diminution in the firing. Ware's Kid crawled down the track, having reloaded his carbine. With his first shot a man cried out shrilly. He pumped the lever and—his carbine jammed. He spat a bitter curse. He knew instantly what had happened—he had slipped a .45 pistol cartridge into a .44 carbine.

A huge shape hurled itself at him. Mechanically he threw up his carbine, and the oncoming man ran into it. Then Ware's Kid, tugging at the butt of his seldom-used Colt, leaped aside. A roar sounded, almost in his ear. Then a hand caught his shoulder. Instinctively he stepped close to his assailant, turned like a flash when a pistol brushed him, dropped his Colt, and caught the fellow's gun hand with both of his and hung on grimly.

"Somethin's wrong, boys! Let's git out o' yere!" a cool, half-laughing voice was shouting, down the track—not the voice that had called Simp Dunbar's name.

The fellow with whom Ware's Kid grappled was swinging terrific blows at his light opponent. But the ranger's head was against his chest; the big fellow's fists but grazed their mark. Ware was tiring with his bulldog grip on the other's gun hand. Suddenly he released his hold and tried to leap backward. A heel caught on a bunch of grass, and he stumbled. A flash and roar from in front of him, a stinging pain across his head. He crashed flat.

He came to, conscious of a dull headache and, next, of a dim light over his head. After a moment of thinking, he perceived that he was sitting in a chair of a railway coach. Next he realized that the train was moving.

"How d'you-all feel now?" inquired an anxious voice.

Painfully he turned his head and saw Bos Johnson's worried face opposite him.

"Right puny," he grunted truthfully.

Johnson grinned widely, relief in his brown eyes.

"What happened?" demanded Ware's Kid.

"Bullet creased you-all. You-all been pickin' daisies might' nigh a hour."

"The hell! Where we going? Gang get away?"

"Going into Dallas. Yeah, gang high-tailed it . . . all but Simp Dunbar," said Johnson. "Reckon they'll 'most all be a-lickin' some sore spots, though. Me 'n' you-all did right smart o' shootin'. I hollered fer Simp an' like a damn' jughead. He spoke right up. I snuck up onto him an' told him who I was."

He lifted his arm and in the loose flannel of his shirt beneath it showed a great hole with charred edges.

"Might' nigh got me, first crack. But I worked buttonholes up an' down his front 'fore he could shoot ag'in."

"How come you found me?"

"By lookin' around," shrugged Johnson affectionately. "You damn' red-eyed li'l runt! You-all think I'd hike out an' leave you-all out there, some'r's fer the gang, mebbe, to find? I come runnin' up about the time you-all tumbled . . . seen that hairpin right on top . . . an' me with an empty gun. I yelled like a Comanche an' damned if he neveh broke an' run."

Ware's Kid eyed him steadily. He knew that only Johnson's arrival had kept his assailant from putting another bullet into him as he lay unconscious. He leaned back wearily in the seat. Johnson stretched his bowed legs comfortably and took off his Stetson.

"Wisht I had a chaw," he grumbled.

"Got the makin's." Ware's Kid fumbled in his jumper pocket.

"Don't use her that-a-way. I neveh could learn to smoke some way."

He threw his head back and closed his eyes. And the ranger, watching him, turned suddenly cold all over. For upon the brown, sinewy neck that had been always hidden heretofore by the silken neckerchief shone a long white scar that stretched evenly three quarters of the way around it. A stocky, dark-faced, dark-eyed man with a white scar circling evenly around his neck—so Simeon Rutter and the O-Bar hands had described Dell Spreen. True, they had seen him clean-shaven, and, believing him guilty of murder, they remembered his features and eyes as murderous. But there was no doubt about it—Dell Spreen sat there across from him with closed eyes. And to Dell Spreen he owed his life that night.

"Dell Spreen," he called in a low voice.

Bos Johnson moved like a cat to half draw his Colt. Then he saw the Derringer that covered him with twin barrels. For an instant he hesitated, then shoved the Colt back into its holster and slumped.

"So you-all come afteh *me*," he said. "I been lookin' fer somebody to show up. That's why I got me a job as dep'ty. Figgered whoever come'd spill his tale in the office an', seein' me wearin' a badge, wouldn't suspicion me. 'Specially since I neveh used my own name in the O-Bar country. But you-all shore fooled me."

"Hate like hell to do it." Ware's Kid wriggled miserably. "But I'm a Texas Ranger. Do anything I can to help you, Johnson. Much as I'd do for my own blood kin. But I got to take you back."

"I ain't blamin' you-all. But . . . might's well shoot me right now, as to put me up 'fore a jury in that country. Ever'thing's ag'inst me . . . 'specially bein' a strangeh. That's why I high-tailed it soon's I heerd he'd been found. I ain't denyin' I went to the O-Bar figgerin' I'd mebbe have to kill Carson. I was goin' to git back the money he stole offen my brotheh and sisteh. Goin' to git it back or try the case before ol' Jedge Colt. But if I'd killed him, it'd been from the front. He'd have been give a chance to fill his hand."

"You . . . you mean you never killed him?" queried Ware's Kid. Then the old surge of hope died. Of course, Johnson would say that.

"D'you-all figger me that-a-way? Knowin' no more about me than you do?" Johnson asked.

Slowly the ranger shook his head.

"Looky yere," argued the deputy. "Eph Carson an' my brotheh, Sam, they was ranchin' it oveh on the Brazos. Carson's a tough *hombre,* remember. He's gamblin' a lot. Well, he sells ever' last head o' stuff on the place while Sam's down in Fort Worth. Time Sam gits back with my kid sisteh that's got a share in the ranch, Carson's done gambled away the money. They's a row, o' course. Sam, he's got more guts than gun sense. Carson nigh kills him.

"Time I come into it, Carson's rattled his hocks. Two years afteh, I'm ridin' down in the El Paso country. Hear about Eph Carson o' the O-Bar. I go high-tailin' it oveh an' hang around four, five days, but Carson don't come. Then I start out fer Crow Point a-huntin' him.

"Then, hell-bent, comes the Mex cook's helper boy. I kept a cowboy from beatin' him to death one day. Says Carson's killed an' robbed, an' ever'body says I must've killed him. Well, whut do I do? Try to tell them red-eyed O-Bar boys as how I was intendin' to kill Eph Carson, mebbe, but neveh got no chanct? Like hell! I figger the job I come to do is done. I leave that 'ere country in a mile-high cloud o' dust."

Ware's Kid slumped lower in the seat, going over and over his mental picture of the scene of the crime.

Bos Johnson rose to cup his hands against the window glass and peer out into the night. Missing no slightest movement of his prisoner, the ranger studied again the wide, powerful shoulders, the bandy legs of the man who had ridden almost since birth. Johnson turned slowly. "Dallas. Be in soon," he said. "Then . . . I ain't blamin' you-all none, Ware. But just . . . well, sort o' between us, I wisht I could make you believe I never done it. I sort o' took to you-all from the beginnin' an'. . . ."

" 'Tain't a bit of use," interrupted Ware's Kid. A tiny smile was born far back in the gray-green eyes, seemed to spread over the habitually blank brown face, and come finally to rest upon the thin-lipped mouth. " 'Tain't a bit of use," he repeated, "because I know you never done it."

Ostentatiously he returned the Derringer to his jumper pocket.

" 'S all right, Bos. You got to go down to Austin with me. Got to exhibit you some to the adjutant general to make him *sabe*. But that'll be all. Listen. I went snoopin' around some myself, down at Carwell. Found where the fella that killed Eph Carson had waited. Point one. There were two brown cigarette stubs on the ground. You-all say you don't smoke, and there's no stain on your fingers.

"I found where this fella stood with his rifle in a sort of notch. His footprints were still pretty plain. Well, your feet, Bos, point in, like a pigeon's. This fella's showed in the soft dirt under the rock overhang, a-pointin' out! But point three's the big one. I stand five foot, seven, and that notch he rested his Winchester in was level with my eyes. Short as you-all are, it'd be mighty near over your head. Now, he never stood on nothing, because there isn't anything there to stand on. And he never fired from no saddle because I found where his horse'd been tied back in the brush."

"Man, but you-all shore wiped some cold sweat offen me," replied Bos Johnson. "I knowed I neveh done it, but provin' it, the way you-all just done, neveh would've come to me, I reckon."

"Took a bigger man than ary one of us. That's what we're goin' to show the adjutant general. Then I'm going to ask him to let me go back to Carwell to find the fella that really did the killin'. He'll let me go. An'. . . ."

"If he does," interrupted Bos Johnson, "they's shore some six-footehs down in that Carwell country as'll be up in the air two ways to onct."

Up out of the glaring yellow sand, the long, low, narrow barrier of black rock jutted abruptly. El Castillo—The Castle—the Mexicans had named it long ago. The name fitted as well as such names usually do. Actually it more resembled a stone fence fifty yards long which, in height, varied from three to ten feet and, in thickness from a foot to four, even five, feet. The top was jagged—sharp saw teeth of slick, inky rock—a sinister pile, even in the white sunlight of a desert afternoon.

Ware's Kid squatted on spurred heels at The Castle's western end, where the trail forked to run on either side of the wall. Not much of a trail, this—the deep, loose, perpetually drifting sand soon effaced impressions—but generations of travel had made a lane between walls of greasewood and catclaw and cactus. It was near the ranger's position on this dimly marked track that Eph Carson had died—shot from the saddle without a chance to return the murderer's fire.

Having left Dell Spreen in the care of the adjutant general in Austin and returning swiftly to Carwell, Ware's Kid had come without being observed to the scene of the murder. Now that he knew Spreen had not committed the killing, he must decide who did. *Satisfied the adjutant general Spreen never done it,* reflected the ranger, *but I've got to figure out who did. Spreen's too little. A good-size* hombre *plugged Eph Carson.*

He got up, and the great black stallion that had stood behind him as he squatted now followed like a dog to the spot where Eph Carson's murderer had lain in wait. Ware's Kid knew the place well. *Fella leaned up against the rock right here,* he reënacted the scene mentally. *Lined his sights on Carson. Carson was coming up the other side from over Crow Point way. Fella drilled him plumb center. Went out and took seven thousand out of Carson's saddlebags. Stood right here. Standing on the ground. No horse tracks closer'n that catclaw yonder. Good-size fella. Had to be, to rest his rifle in that crotch.*

Mechanically he studied the rock wall and the sand that swept away from its foot. There was something bright in the sand at the very spot where they had found the murderer's tracks. He stooped. But it was only a glassy bit of rock. He held it, staring absently, his mind upon the mystery. From the little sand dunes behind him, to northward, came the flat, vicious report of a rifle. A bullet slapped the rock wall almost in his face. It had passed within six inches of his head. Instantly another followed.

Ware's Kid moved like a rattler striking, automatically, but with a precision, an economy of movement, that could not have been bettered by rehearsals times without number. He was sheltered from the bullets within two steps, standing behind his stallion's bulk. His hand slapped the saddle horn. He was in the saddle without touching stirrups and lying flat upon the black's neck. The great rowels dug the stallion's flanks; he surged forward magnificently; within two strides he was galloping. The ranger, chased by bullets that buzzed spitefully about his ears, swung the black around the end of The Castle.

Halfway down the length of the stone wall he slid the stallion to a halt. Here was a place where he could peer across the top between two teeth of rock. His great sombrero hung down his back by the chin strap; from the scabbard beneath the left fender had leaped a sleek Winchester carbine. He cuddled the carbine in the crook of his arm as, with green-gray eyes squinting coldly, he studied the sand dunes behind which his antagonist lay hidden.

A thin smoke cloud was drifting upward above the dunes. Ware's Kid rested the carbine in the crotch of the wall top. He sighted carefully and drove three .44s to dust along the crest of the dunes, some fifteen inches apart. Instantly the other rifleman replied with a rolling quartet of bullets that bunched most efficiently beneath the ranger's carbine-muzzle.

He watched narrowly without replying in kind. At last he shrugged and whirled the stallion, to ride off south and east toward the O-Bar ranch house.

He could have stalked the sand dunes from which the unknown bushwhacker had fired. There was cover of a sort up to the very base of the dunes. But the ambusher's fire had been entirely too craftsman-like, too nearly deadly, to make the prospect of scaling the low slope before him seem anything but the brief preliminary to a funeral. Ware's Kid preferred to ride off with a whole skin and calculate upon another meeting under conditions more equal. They said of him, in the Texas Rangers, that for a youngster no more than nineteen he had a mighty level head.

A half mile, perhaps, he galloped without turning. Then, reaching for the field glasses, he checked the stallion. Far behind him, a horseman streaked eastward. The ranger studied rider and brown horse through the glasses. *Maybe he's tall,* he thought, *or maybe he's just forking a little pony.*

For ten miles he kept the stallion at a mile-eating running-walk. He had never been at the O-Bar Ranch, but he knew its location from hearsay, and so, when the black stallion began climbing a steady incline, studded by boulders and covered with taller-than-ordinary mesquite, he nodded to himself. This was the way, all right.

The stallion made the incline's top and paused for a moment, expelling his breath in a great snort. At the sound, the flaxen-haired girl on the look-out rock turned sharply. She and Ware's Kid stared, one at another, her great, dark eyes meeting his narrowed gaze levelly.

"Howdy," he drawled, after a—to him—long and uncomfortable silence. He was always ill-at-ease with women. They usually wanted a man to make some sort of damned fool of himself to suit a feminine whim.

"Good morning," she replied, still examining him calmly.

"Trail to the O-Bar?" he asked awkwardly, after another silence.

"Yes. The house is a mile away. But there's nobody there

except the cook and his helper. Do you want to see my father, Sim Rutter?"

Ware's Kid stared. He recalled nothing about a daughter on the O-Bar. And that Simeon Rutter, huge, gaunt, black-haired, black-eyed, black-bearded, grim, and taciturn, should have such a daughter as this slim, fair-skinned creature seemed somehow unbelievable. She seemed to read his thoughts.

"I've been away at school . . . Las Cruces . . . convent, you know," she enlightened. "But I'm not going back . . . I hope."

"Stay here, huh?"

"I hope not! This is just as bad. Oh, I hate this bare, desolate country. Don't you?"

"Don't know," shrugged Ware's Kid. He had never thought about the matter, one way or the other. "Don't know . . . as I do."

"I want to go back East. To New York . . . Philadelphia . . . Boston . . . oh, all the places I've read about. Europe, too. I'm trying to get my father to sell the ranch and to travel with me. All over the world. I've been trying to persuade him for two years. But I think he'll do it, now . . . maybe. His partner was killed, you know. He was all broken up over that. He doesn't say much, but it was an awful blow just the same. I think he'll sell out."

"Got to be going," said Ware's Kid. All this talk of travel was over his head, and it had nothing to do with his particular business—the capture of Eph Carson's murderer.

"I'll ride with you. Will you get my horse? He's tied to a catclaw over yonder."

The ranger got the pony and brought it back. He sat his stallion, holding her animal's reins. She waited for an instant, but he was blind to her expectation that he would help her into the saddle. So she swung up unaided and jerked the reins from his hand.

As they rode almost stirrup to stirrup toward the ranch house, Ware studied her covertly from beneath half-lowered sombrero brim. It dawned upon him suddenly that not yet had he seen her smile. The large blue eyes were somber, always; she seemed to brood about something. They rode in silence until, a half mile or so ahead, the clutter of buildings that constituted the O-Bar holding showed against the desert shrubbery.

"I hate it!" she burst out. "Oh, how I hate it!"

Then they rode on silently again, the creak of saddle leather, the scuffing of the animals' hoofs the only sounds, until they dismounted in the ranch yard. There was but one horse in the cottonwood-log corral, a black gelding as large as the mount of Ware's Kid. The girl glanced at it, then toward the house.

"My father's home," she said tonelessly. "Come in."

They went around the house and, upon the rough verandah that shaded its front, found Simeon Rutter with feet cocked upon the rail, big, shaggy head upon his chest. He looked up at the sound of their footsteps, and sun-narrowed black eyes softened amazingly as he saw his daughter.

"Hello, baby," he rumbled. "Wonderin' where yuh was." Then to Ware's Kid: "Howdy, Kid. What're yuh doin' down here ag'in? Thought they sent yuh up to Austin, or some'r's."

"Did. Sent me back. I got Dell Spreen."

"Yuh did! That's shore good hearin', Kid!" He came swiftly to his feet, with great hands hard-clenched.

The girl had gone indoors, and bitterly, yet with a certain grim repression, Simeon Rutter cursed Dell Spreen. "Where's Spreen now?" he demanded, breaking off suddenly. "Carwell? El Paso?"

"Austin. Looking up some more evidence."

Simeon Rutter cursed the law's dawdling ways, its coddling of an assassin. Ware's Kid but half listened. He was thinking of the efficient rifleman of the morning who had bushwhacked him from the sand dunes.

"How many big men in this country?" he asked abruptly. "*Big* men?"

Rutter stopped short to stare at him. Then he considered the question, eyes narrowed thoughtfully. "Don't know. Me, o' course. An' Curly Gonzales over Crow Point way. Lamson . . . that crazy 'puncher on the D-Five . . . an' Slim Nichols on the Flyin' A. All I think of. Why?"

The ranger hesitated. Knowing Rutter's bitterness toward Dell Spreen, he wondered if the dour ranchman could be made to believe his own theory: that Spreen had not, could not have, committed the murder. He wondered, too, if Rutter would be silent about the theory. "Spreen says he never killed Carson," he said slowly.

"Yeah. An' what?"

"And if he did . . . well, I don't know how he did it."

"What're yuh drivin' at?" Yuh got the name o' bein' level-headed, Kid, but . . . what're yuh drivin' at?"

"How could a little fella . . . littler'n me . . . shoot Carson, resting his gun in a crotch near as high as he could reach?"

Scowling, Simeon Rutter considered this problem. "That *was* a high crotch . . . the one we found his tracks under," he admitted. "But, hell! He was sittin' on a hoss, or else standin' on somethin'. Not good enough, Kid! By God, not half good enough to make me believe Dell Spreen never shot old Eph Carson from hidin'. O' course, he denies it! 'Spect him to own right up?"

"Yes. 'Course, he'd say he didn't, but I've been thinking. Weren't any horse tracks under the crotch. Nothing to stand on. Nothing we could see, anyhow. So, I wondered who'd be tall enough to shoot out of that crotch, standing on the sand. And, too. . . ." He hesitated for an instant before he decided to tell of the morning. "And, too, somebody bushwhacked me out at The Castle today."

"Bushwhacked you? What for? Who'd be a-bushwhackin' you?"

"Don't know. Fella on a dun. Good shot, too. Purty good, that is."

"Here!" cried Rutter suddenly. "Too much funny business about this. I want to see that place ag'in. Git yo' hoss, Kid. Let's take a *pasear* out to The Castle an' look around."

He went swiftly down to the corral and got the lariat from his saddle. The black gelding retreated to a corner, snorting, whirling. Rutter sent the loop spinning over its head and hauled the animal to him by sheer brute force.

"So damn' many hosses none gits rid enough," he rumbled irritably. "Wilder'n antelope, all of 'em."

He saddled swiftly and swung up. Ware's Kid was already mounted. They turned past the front verandah, and Rutter waved to his daughter, who had come outside again. He seemed another person when near her. The grim shell of him cracked, and a tenderness odd in a man so apparently harsh-grained showed for a moment.

"Goin' out to El Castillo!" he shouted at the girl. "Back when I git back, baby."

They rode silently for miles. Rutter was one after the ranger's own heart, taciturn, efficient in his business. Staring at his companion's broad back, Ware nodded approval. He thought of what the girl had said—of her father's repressed sorrow over his partner's death. He could understand Rutter's vengefulness toward Dell Spreen, but he hoped, before the day's end, to show the O-Bar owner his error, to prove that Spreen could not have murdered Eph Carson.

"If yuh're right about this height business," Rutter growled suddenly, "I don't know what we're goin' to do about it. Too long ago, now. Not that I'm admittin' yuh're right! But, just in case yuh are, how can we find out where these fellas . . . Curly Gonzales an' Lamson an' Nichols . . . was that day? Fella don't always recollect just what he was doin' three months ago. By George!" He whirled sideways in the saddle. "That mornin', me an' August Koenig . . . one o' my hands . . . was ridin' nawth o' the house nine, ten mile. An' we met Lamson headin' for Elizario. Recollect now, August an' Lamson come near mixin' it, 'count August, he was askin' about some widder that lives in Elizario an' Lamson flew off the handle. By George."

"What kind of fella's Lamson?" inquired Ware.

"Oh, same's most. Gits kind o' crazy spells. Been kicked on the head a long time ago by a bronc', an' once in a while he flies up. But he's a good 'puncher, an' I don't know why anybody'd think he'd shoot Eph Carson. Lamson's seen trouble . . . seen it fair and square, through the smoke. No-o, I wouldn't put him down for that kind o' killer."

"You found Carson right after noon, didn't you?"

"Yeah. I got fidgety, him not comin' in the day I figgered. So, when me an' August got back to the house, an' Eph hadn't come in yet, I took August an' Yavapai Wiggins, an' we rode out. Found Eph 'long about two o'clock, lyin' in the trail. Seven thousand, about, he was packin'. All gone."

"Mostly yours, they say."

" 'Bout four thousand," Rutter nodded gloomily. "But it wasn't the money riled me so. Old Eph, he never knowed what hit him. Never had a chanct. Nary chanct to git his six-shooter out. Like I told yuh then, right after it happened, I

figgered Dell Spreen 'cause he'd hung around the ranch three
days, waitin' for Eph. Wouldn't tell nobody what he wanted.
Just looked mean. An' packed his *cantinas* an' high-tailed it
that very mawnin'. I gethered yuh never found the money on
him?"

"Four dollars, about," shrugged Ware's Kid.

They came to The Castle and reined in the animals on the
spot where the murderer of Eph Carson had waited. Silently
Simeon Rutter stared at the crotch in the rock wall in which
the assassin had rested his rifle barrel. Slowly, as unwilling
even now to concede weight to the theory the ranger had ad-
vanced tentatively, he nodded.

"They wasn't no hoss tracks closer'n that catclaw
yonder," he admitted.

He swung down and pulled his Winchester from its scabbard, then moved over to the crotch in the wall. Even for one
of his height it was a strain to level the barrel with butt at
shoulder. He nodded again and set the rifle down. From a
shirt pocket he brought Durham and papers and shook tobacco onto the brown leaf, somber black eyes roving.

Ware's Kid slipped from the saddle and came swiftly over
to where Rutter stood. He stopped and dug into the sand at
the rancher's feet, then straightened.

"What is it?" asked Rutter.

It was a large, pearl-handled pocket knife, tarnished from
much carrying, with four good blades and one broken blade
stump. Rutter licked his cigarette, jammed it into his mouth,
and took the knife from the ranger's hand, staring thoughtfully.

"See it before?" asked Ware's Kid.

Rutter shook his head. "Umm . . . no, reckon not. Not
many like that carried in this country. But somebody ought to
know it. We'll ride into Carwell pretty soon. See. But right

now I want to ride Eph Carson's back trail. Got a idee. Mebbe she won't pan out."

They could only guess that Eph Carson had come along the regular trail and followed through the dim lane between the greasewood and cacti. They rode silently, with eyes roving from trail to skyline and back again. The afternoon wore on; evening came. To westward, upthrusting hills, jagged, fantastic, drew nearer.

"Huecos," grunted Rutter, and Ware's Kid nodded. He knew this ancient watering place of the desert people, red and brown and white. A good many times, with a ranger detachment from Ysleta hunting Apache sign, he had camped there.

"Guess we better hole up there t'night," Rutter grunted, staring across the flat to the beginning of that welter of arroyo-cut hillocks. "Mawnin' we can head back to Carwell an' see 'bout that frog-sticker. Or, we can look over some more trail."

"Your idea?" queried Ware's Kid. "You said you had one."

"Tell yuh about it come mawnin'," said Rutter. Far back in the grim black eyes lurked a shadowy amusement. "Ain't quite ready to back her up clean to the tailgate. Got anything to eat?"

"Dried beef, tortillas, coffee, can of plums."

"Dried beef an' tortillas is a meal," grinned Rutter. "Le's head for the tanks an' camp."

"Better hole up in the old Butterfield station," counseled Ware's Kid. "Healthier sleeping alongside the main *tinaja*. Apaches still don't stick close to the reservation, I reckon."

"Not so close, by God!" swore Rutter. "Yuh're right, Kid. Them damn' feather-dusters stops here or at Crow Springs or the Cornudas, reg'lar, comin' from Mescalero to Chihuahua. Stage station she is. We'll make it."

83

They nodded mutual agreement and spurred the horses on through the dark. At the deserted stage station—a rude dwelling made by walling in the mouth of a natural cavern—they swung down. The ranger sniffed like a hunting dog.

"Some seep water up the cañon a piece," he muttered. "Good enough for the hosses. But I'll take the canteen and get some real water at the tank for us."

He unsaddled the black stallion, and swiftly Rutter followed his example. Rutter got out the food and coffee pot from the ranger's saddlebags while the latter, bearing a canteen, started up the cañon to the main tank.

Ware's Kid moved silently, for all his high-heeled boots. The cañon floor was of hard-packed earth but studded with loose stones, and he placed his feet carefully. One never knew who might be using the tanks. From time immemorial it had been one of the favorite watering places of this region. Wild animals and wild men, red and brown and white, came here furtively.

He passed close along the left-hand wall, decorated with Indian pictographs and the names of pioneers, and so came to the low cavern in which was the spring-fed well, or tank. More cautiously than ever he moved now. The rock apron before the cavern was pitted with *metate* holes where prehistoric tribes had ground their corn, rude mortars still used by the Apaches who camped here. It was tricky footing and trickier still inside, where one approached the well lip over a stone floor worn slick as glass by countless feet.

Inside the cavern mouth he squatted for a moment and listened. He heard nothing from without or within and slid his feet carefully forward, balancing himself with left hand upon a rounded slab that divided the cavern in two sections. So he was awkwardly balanced when a sinewy arm shot around his throat from behind and a—*Hough!*—sounded in his ear. A smallish, rather insignificant-seeming figure was Ware's Kid. But all whalebone and whang leather, as the rangers who had wrestled with him remarked amazedly, a hundred and ten pounds of wiry, flashingly quick, steel-strong body. Now he moved automatically, fairly shouting: "Indians!" Sideways he whirled, and so the Apache's knife went wide in its downward drive. Back shot the ranger's head, to smash into the Indian's face. It broke the strangling hold, and Ware's Kid, turning half in air, his feet were sliding so, shot a vicious fist into the Apache's midriff, then had the buck by the throat, and was gripping him about the body with legs closing like scissors-blades and fending off flailing arms with elbows spread.

The Apache was powerful, but, before he had much opportunity to struggle, Ware's Kid had banged his head back against the rock. The Indian managed a long, loud, gasping groan. Feebly his knife hand rose. The ranger loosed the throat for an instant and fumbled for the weapon. It sliced his palm. Then he seized it and buried it in the Indian's body.

When the Apache was limp—wise men made very sure that Apaches were really dead—the ranger stood up shakily and groped for the entrance. A stone slid down into the cañon, and he hurled himself forward out of the cavern. As he gained the middle of the cañon, running like a quarter horse, there was thud after thud of feet dropping from the rocks to the hard ground. He ran on his toes, hoping that he could make camp sufficiently ahead of these fleet Indians to warn Rutter, hoping, too, that Rutter had the horses together, had not taken them out onto the flat to graze. He ran as he never had run in his life. At last he sensed the camp just ahead. And from it came a rifle shot, then another. The bullets sang past him, perilously close.

"It's . . . Ware's Kid!" he gasped. "Indians . . . coming!"

"Thought yuh was one of 'em," grunted Rutter, with no particular alarm evident in his heavy voice. "How close?"

"Right behind! No time to saddle! Fork 'em bareback!"

He paused only to snatch his precious carbine from its scabbard on the saddle, then scooped up the bight of the lariat with which the stallion was picketed. He vaulted upon the stallion's back. Muffled sound in the darkness nearby told that Rutter was following his example.

Up the cañon the darkness was suddenly punctuated in a half dozen places by orange flames. Bullets thudded into the ground, into rock walls, around the white men. The firing was a continuous roll, its rumbling multiplied by the cañon walls. As usual the Apaches had rifles as good as any in that country, better than those of the Army. Rutter swore venomously.

Ware's Kid had slashed the lariat with his belt knife. Rutter, apparently, had done the same. For when the black stallion surged ahead, toward the safety of the open land, Rutter was close behind. They galloped furiously for perhaps half an hour. The moon came out and flooded the desert with a white light that reminded the ranger of Billy Conant's New Fashion Saloon in El Paso when the electric lights were turned on.

Being lighter and, perhaps, the better rider, Ware's Kid led. He had lost a hundred-dollar saddle, but he was phlegmatic about that. It was all in the game. They were lucky—he especially—to be riding away with their hair. A sudden groan from Rutter aroused him from his thoughts, and he looked backward under his arm in time to see the big man slide sideways off his gelding and roll over upon his side.

Mechanically Ware's Kid whirled the stallion and glared half a dozen ways at once in search of the assassin. But the broad expanse of greasewood and cacti lay quietly in the incandescent moonlight. So he rode back to Rutter and slid to the sand.

"Got me," Rutter gasped. "Back yonder. Thought I . . . could make it . . . back to the ranch . . . see . . . my girl . . . but. . . ."

"Let's see," grunted Ware's Kid practically.

He explored the blood-caked shirt front and lifted a shoulder point in a little gesture of fatalistic resignation. There was a .44 hole in Rutter's chest. How he had ridden this far was the marvel! The ranger squatted there broodingly, watching along the back trail in case the Indians appeared.

"Want me to . . . sign a paper?"

At the painful whisper, Ware's Kid looked down curiously into Rutter's grim-outlined face. "Sure," he nodded after a moment, thinking to humor a delirious man. "If it'll ease you."

"Knowed yuh . . . had the deadwood on me . . . when yuh . . . found my knife. But I . . . wasn't goin' to . . . let yuh see Carwell ag'in . . . ever. Yuh tried to . . . make out yuh never . . . suspicioned. But I knowed. I'd've got yuh . . . yeste'day mawnin'. Damn' near got yuh . . . yeste'day mawnin' . . . at The Castle. Seen yuh . . . pokin' 'round . . . pick up somethin' . . . skeered me an' . . . I whanged away. Hadn't missed . . . wouldn't be here. 'Twas in the . . . cards . . . I reckon."

He stopped wearily, breathing in labored wheezes. Ware's Kid squatted beside him, staring down with expressionless face. Suddenly Rutter's wheezes became louder, quicker. After a moment the ranger understood that it was horrible laughter.

"Reckon my gal . . . will do her travelin' . . . now. Always after me . . . to sell out. I done for Eph Carson . . . 'count o' that. None o' that money was mine. All his'n. I wanted it. I. . . ."

Eugene Cunningham

His voice trailed off into incoherent mumbling. Ware's Kid bethought himself suddenly of what Rutter had said about signing a paper. He fumbled in his jumper pocket and found a letter of the adjutant general's, the letter that had summoned him to Austin three months ago and so had brought him, indirectly, to sit here tonight. A stub of pencil was there, too.

"All right," he snapped. "Sign the paper."

He supported the murderer's head and shoulders and crooked his knee so that Rutter could lay the paper upon it. It was slow, painful work, but at last he held the curt scrawl up in the moonlight and painfully spelled it out:

Dell Spreen never killed eph Carson I done it and robbed him. Simeon Rutter.

Presently Rutter died—without pain apparently. Ware's Kid rolled a cigarette and lit it, staring blankly straight ahead. *He sure fooled me,* he thought admiringly. *He sure did. And almost killed me twice. At The Castle and tonight. He never took me for no Indian. He was aiming to down me. Just fool's luck I'm here, alive and kicking, and with this here paper.*

He got up, thinking to ride for Carwell and tell his story, show the confession. Suddenly he thought of the girl, the wistful-eyed, sad-faced girl at the O-Bar ranch house. He squatted again and made another cigarette.

Slowly, but surely, he mulled the business over. It came to him finally that there were really but two persons to be considered—Dell Spreen, sitting around the adjutant general's office up at Austin, and that girl of Rutter's. Absolute vindication of Spreen was easy; the means lay in his hand. But that would mean a blow at a girl who had had no part in her father's cold-blooded deed. He pondered the problem. At last, he nodded.

88

He would ride back to Carwell, but the paper would remain in his jumper pocket. He would tell of Rutter's death, lead a posse after the Apaches. He would also show the townsfolk the spot from which Eph Carson had been shot and explain the impossibility of Dell Spreen—a man shorter, even, than himself—committing the murder. This might not clear up the mystery to everyone's satisfaction, but Dell Spreen had no intention of coming back to this part of the country anyway. When the adjutant general saw the confession, it would clear Spreen officially. Then the girl would not be branded—openly, at least—as the daughter of a brutal, callous murderer. She would have no ordeal to face while the O-Bar was being sold. She would carry away no bitter memories to mark her in after years.

Something like this Ware's Kid thought out. He got up again and snapped his fingers to the black stallion, caught the trailing lariat, and again threw a hackamore around the black's nose, then vaulted upon it with carbine across his arm.

Reckon this is poor law . . . this way, he reflected. *But it's sure as hell good rangering!*

The Hammer Thumb

Ware's Kid made the stage station in the half hour before noon. The tall, black stallion halted without signal before the adobe corral from which rose clouds of dust and the sound of men's angry voices. As Ware leaned over the corral wall and peered through the swirling dust, a faint twinkle showed far back in the gray-green eyes that were shaded by the huge, silver-embroidered sombrero. For very evidently a mule was to be shod, and—also very evidently—the mule was registering violent objection. Three men were moving about him cautiously with lariats circling, and, finally caught by three legs, the mule crashed flat.

There were three of them, Ware's Kid noted, where ordinarily there would have been but one. He thought that none of the trio understood the reason for this unusual guarding of the stage line. He himself knew very well, for the reason was the same one that had moved him from the Texas Rangers' camp well before dawn that day. It was only a two-word reason, but those two words had power to lower men's voices, to cause furtive glances over a shoulder, to render nervous even the hard-bitten cowhands over two hundred miles of country. The two words were: Red Sleeves.

He rode usually with two followers, this bandit who struck with such uncanny accuracy at the stages. He never struck at a point where he was expected to appear; the stage he stopped always carried treasure, either in the money box or on the person of some passenger. Having looted it, Red Sleeves and

93

his followers vanished as into thin air. Twice they had left dead men behind them.

One thing only was definitely known about him and that was the result of a deduction on the part of Captain Knowles of the ranger company, a deduction made only a few days before. Checking up on the various details of the half dozen robberies credited to Red Sleeves, a regularity about the interval separating each robbery from the next had impressed Knowles.

Three months, within a very few days, had elapsed each time between the outlaw's activities, and—it now lacked but a couple of days of the time for another robbery. It was this thought that had led Knowles first to warn the stage company to post extra guards and then detail young Ware to search for the elusive Red Sleeves gang. Almost his only clue was knowledge that the bandit leader always wore a red shirt. It was this that had given him his *nom de guerre*.

"Dinner?" inquired the ranger of the three heavily armed men who turned to stare curiously at his Mexican finery, his awkwardly hung white-handled Colt.

They nodded, and the regular stagekeeper went off to the adobe bunkhouse that was built against the mouth of a cave in one of the low hills that marked this little halting place of the stages.

When he had eaten, Ware's Kid rested for a while in the shade of the cabin wall, smoking silently or replying in monosyllables to the remarks of the guards or keeper. Not a word did he hear of Red Sleeves.

The lazy drumming of the stallion's hoofs in the sand roused no apparent interest anywhere upon the dusty street of Las Tunas, walled in by twin lines of low adobes spotted here and there by new brick buildings. Ware's Kid reined in the stallion and gazed thoughtfully down the nearly deserted thoroughfare.

It seemed that every third or fourth adobe upon the street opened into a saloon. There was one on his right, just ahead. Before it stood a battered and reeling hitching post, against which a Mexican youth leaned drowsily with sandaled feet projecting into the path that served as sidewalk.

From this saloon now swaggered a huge, dark man in a broad, black hat, red flannel shirt, and overalls that were thrust into the tops of half boots. He paused for an instant to stare incuriously at the small figure in Mexican clothing sitting the great stallion, then turned to go upstreet—and cruelly trampled the toes of the Mexican youth with high boot heels.

The boy cried out shrilly, staggered sidewise, and fell flat upon his back in the dust. The big man eyed him carelessly from the corner of a black eye—much as if he had been a stick or other unimportant, inanimate thing. The Mexican, from where he lay, glowered at the trampler. A glint of teeth showed wolfishly between his snarling lips. This the big man saw.

"Why, damn yo' yaller soul," he remarked deliberately.

With a single stride he was standing over the Mexican. The heavy quirt looped to his left hand whistled up, then descended with a terrific *whish* to curl about the Mexican's shoulders. The boy couldn't get away, for the big man's boot pinned one hand to the dust. He could only writhe and cringe as the quirt mercilessly rose and fell.

The ranger's lean brown face hardened as he watched. It was a hard time in all the vast Western country, and men were not much moved by ordinary brutality. So it was the cold, passionless manner of the big man that roused in Ware's Kid a slow-rising anger he could not explain. The big man looked up sidewise, without change of expression, as the stallion's shadow fell across him.

"Reckon," drawled the boyish-looking ranger almost gently, "this'll be all."

"Yo' reckonin'," replied the big man without apparent interest, "is plumb out."

Then the quirt leaped up again and once more curled about the Mexican.

To a mountainous, white-haired man in broad straw hat and snowy linens, who was now framed in the saloon doorway, it seemed that half a dozen things occurred simultaneously, with an abruptness that could be likened only to an explosion. The black's shoulder cannoned into the big man with the quirt—the ranger was on the ground—the big man's wrist was seized and twisted deftly—his feet were kicked from under him with what seemed the same movement—his body described a half arc in the air that ended when his face plowed into the dust of the street.

When he scrambled to his haunches—clawing frantically for a Colt that had sailed from its holster—he was promptly knocked down again by a flashing knee that collided with an eye. Still fumbling for the absent gun butt, he was permitted to get to his feet, only to be measured by a stabbing left hand and knocked unconscious by a terrific, looping right.

Two others stood now behind the enormous old man in the saloon door, peering over his shoulders. These elbowed past him, hard-faced men, both. They glanced down at the sprawling figure and back with a sort of curious menace at the easy-postured ranger. They made no hostile move, only stooped, gathered up the senseless one, and staggered inside the saloon with him.

Ware's Kid was reaching for the stallion's reins when the

mountainous white-haired man addressed him in a piping tenor.

"Howdy, son."

Ware's Kid turned a slow head, gray-green eyes probing the old man's guileless red face. Then gravely he nodded.

"That"—the big white head jerked slightly toward the saloon door—"was a right good job . . . but dangerous."

The ranger waited. They faced each other silently, the small figure in short jacket of soft tanned goatskin, loose Mexican-cut trousers of blue woolen, belling over high-heeled boots, and the vast figure in wide straw hat and immaculate linen suit that gleamed so incongruously in the shabby street.

"Come on over to my store, son, if you don't mind. I'd like to talk to you a spell," said the big man.

They crossed the street and entered a new brick building which bore across its front a sign proclaiming general merchandise and announcing Dave Barrow as proprietor. The store, without and within, was like its owner: prosperous-seeming and comfortable and orderly. It was a much more elaborate establishment than Ware's Kid had ever seen before in the range country. Dave Barrow led the way to the rear, and the ranger noted the respect with which the old man was greeted by the dozen or so customers who were being waited upon by several white or Mexican clerks. He began to understand that Dave Barrow was a person of importance in Las Tunas.

Barrow stood aside at the door of a large, pleasantly cool, and dusky room that had been made by a partition stretching from wall to wall of the store itself. There was a huge desk, a few easy chairs, a rack with many newspapers—precious things in that country—and a great bookcase in the corner.

Dave Barrow motioned toward a chair, but Ware's Kid

shook his head and squatted upon his heels against the wall. Likewise he refused a cigar from the red Mexican *olla* in which the storekeeper kept them secure against the penetrating dryness of that latitude. He produced thick yellow-brown papers and inky Mexican tobacco, made a cigarette, lit it with a match from his hatband, and waited, his sagging posture reminiscent of a drowsing cow pony at a hitch rack.

"I'd like to offer you-all a job," said Dave Barrow after a space. He paused and stared thoughtfully at the wall, with rolling chins sunk upon his chest. "Las Tunas right now is in a hell of a fix!" he exploded.

His piping tenor was almost childishly querulous, but Ware's Kid, skilled far beyond his years in the reading of men, sensed a force in the fat man quite in keeping with his great bulk. He waited.

"When we was just a cowtown, certain things was all well enough. But we're goin' to be a city right soon. White folks here sat and prayed . . . all nine of 'em . . . for a railroad. Now, we're goin' to have four railroads. Minute the word spread that buildin' was goin' to begin, we started to get new settlers. Good folks, bad folks, an' indifferent . . . though you would think, to see our two streets at night, that the whole blame' town was just gamblers an' saloonkeepers an' variety girls and that sort of sportin' crowd. They've been tryin' to run Las Tunas. But some of us old-timers got together an' organized a town council. They made me president.

"We built a jail an' we hired a city marshal an' we give him a deputy an' told him to keep the town halfway quiet. But our marshal got to be too good friends with the sportin' crowd. He couldn't make any arrests without tramplin' on his friends' corns. Yesterday mornin' we let him out an' made the deputy actin' marshal. I telegraphed to a man I knew up-country an' offered him the job. He said he'd take it, but it'll be a day or two before he can get here. Last night I found the actin' marshal crazy drunk in Williams's Variety Theater an' I fired him right there. So . . . tonight Las Tunas will have no police force.

"Nobody knows about my telegraphin' my friend. Son, we're sure in a fix tonight. The sportin' crowd is goin' to shoot us up. They're goin' to prove to the town council that Las Tunas needs a two-gun marshal . . . needs Louis Sanders. But, whilst they're a-doin' this provin', some grudges are naturally goin' to be settled. Some folks'll be killed. Some more'll be hurt right bad. Property belongin' to the decent folks'll be kindlin' wood tomorrow, if. . . . Son, will you take the job as deputy marshal . . . actin' marshal until my man gets here? When I saw you clean Louis Sanders's plow, I thought to myself . . . here's the man that's the answer to the question I've been askin' myself all day."

"Who's Louis Sanders?" inquired Ware.

"He *was* the marshal. Will you help us out, son? Will you take a job as deputy marshal?"

Ware's Kid shook his head. "Can't," he said. "Against the law."

Dave Barrow's broad red face grew sorrowful.

"But," said Ware's Kid, "you can call on me to ride herd on the town, if you want to . . . for I'm a ranger, you see?"

Las Tunas' two principal streets formed a capital T. North Street, some six blocks long, was the top bar; East Street, a little longer, formed the vertical staff. Evidently word of the humbling of Louis Sanders had gone on wings about Las Tunas, for Ware's Kid, looking the town over thoughtfully that afternoon, was conscious of stares more numerous, more curious than warranted by his Mexican clothing, the white-handled Colt hung awkwardly high, or the sleek carbine cuddled in his arm. But his blank face showed no sign that he noticed, as he studied the geography of Las Tunas in detail.

He came presently to the Three Jacks Saloon at the far extremity of East Street—the saloon outside of which he had met Sanders. He was passing with eyes roving slowly when he noted that in the gray dust around the hitch post the traces of Sanders's several falls had not been effaced. A couple of loungers in the saloon doorway eyed him with cold calculation while he stood staring at the ruffled dust.

He turned after a moment, staring at them expressionlessly but to remember, then went on at his awkward, high-heeled horseman's gait across the street and back toward the center of town. As he went, his eyes were narrowed thoughtfully and far back in their gray-green depths was shining an odd, cold light that, with him, marked anticipation of swiftest action. His thin mouth was lifted a little at one corner in the faintest of shadowy smiles.

The marshal's office was only a tiny room in the new brick jail that stood perhaps a hundred feet off North Street. There was a Chinese restaurant at the corner of the little side street leading to the jail. Here Ware's Kid ate a large supper, then strolled down to the office. He found two ten-gauge shotguns with sawed-off barrels leaning in a corner. These he inspected, then regretfully hid his carbine in a pile of odds and ends in one corner, and picked up the shotguns. With both of them across his arm he went back up to North Street. At one corner of the intersection of North and East Streets was the great Criterion Saloon and gambling room. Next door to it was a hardware store, in the door of which stood a bare-headed, lean, bitter-faced, one-legged man. Ware's Kid crossed the street and nodded to this man. He had seen that the sign announced the proprietor as John Curran.

"Boss?" he asked.

After a long, probing stare, the bare-headed man nodded. "Complete," he grunted. "I'm Curran. You're the ranger. What can I do for you?"

"Shells," said Ware's Kid briefly, when they stood inside the dusky, crowded store.

Curran nodded, glanced at the shotguns, then went stomping behind the counter, his wooden leg clumping against the floor with an angry sound as if with each step he voiced his resentment at being crippled. "No damages," he snapped, when he had laid a box of ten-gauge shells before the ranger. Again he favored Ware's Kid with that long, probing stare. Then, suddenly, he whirled and pulled down a large cardboard box, opened it, and produced a queer-looking vest of light calfskin to the sides of which were sewed pistol holsters. "Take off your jumper," he commanded, and, after a moment of hesitation, Ware's Kid obeyed. "Put this on!"

Ware's Kid slipped his arms through the vest, and the merchant, bending forward across the counter, buckled the vest together. The two holsters rested now beneath Ware's arms. From the high-hung belt holster he drew his seldom-used Colt and shoved it into one of the holsters of the vest. It hung at a canny slant. Curran grunted again and whirled for another box, from which he produced the mate to the ranger's six-shooter and shoved it into the second holster.

"Now!" he snarled. "That's the John Wesley Hardin quick-draw outfit. You cross your arms as you draw. Practice a little and you can be chain lightning."

Ware's Kid shook his head slowly, a trifle regretfully, staring down at the outfit. "Some other time, maybe. Right now . . . not enough money."

"Who asked you for money?" snarled Curran. "Reckon I belong to the town council, same as Dave Barrow. Reckon I

can appreciate your sticking around to buck the whole town.
Here, load that other gun. You'll likely need it before
morning."

From Dave Barrow, Ware had received rapid-fire thumbnail sketches of the town prominents, so he knew that the
Williams brothers were fomenters of everything evil in Las
Tunas; that Joe Billings, who owned the Criterion, was la-
beled one in the confidence neither of such belligerent
leaders of the sporting crowd as the Williams brothers nor
that of the town council; and Hook-Hand Terry, owner of the
Congress Saloon, was a man to tie to. Ware's Kid went,
neither slow nor fast, up East Street to the Congress Saloon.
The streets were beginning to fill with a leisurely, flashily
dressed throng. Gamblers there were, by the dozen almost, in
broad hats, funereal frock coats, gaudy waistcoats, and
mirror-bright boots; the shrill voices of heavily rouged
women in brilliant low-cut silk dresses—each well-squired;
slinking, furtive figures that seemed to trail like coyotes at the
heels of taller members of the half world; cowmen and their
'punchers stumping along awkwardly—like Ware's Kid—on
high boot-heels; bearded miners, usually in knots of two or
three. Ware's Kid drew curious, oft-times menacing glances
from many of those he passed. Eyes flickered from the twin
shotguns across his arm to lean, blank face—then back again.

At the door of the Congress Saloon, he paused for a swift
glance at the crowd inside. At the long bar's end was visible
Hook-Hand Terry himself—a huge man, his bullet head
nearly bald, with red bull throat constricted by a shiny rubber
collar and a diamond the size of a filbert twinkling in his vast
shirt front. Hook-Hand's bare elbows rested upon the bar;
the iron hook—substitute for the left hand lost in some ancient, unnamed naval battle—gripped absently by a ham-like

right fist that was intricately tattooed almost to the finger-nails.

Ware's Kid came inside and down the barroom. The saloonkeeper's small blue eyes narrowed for an instant at sight of the ranger's burden, then he smiled and nodded approvingly.

"Sure, ut's quite a battery ye have, me son!" he boomed.

"Want to leave a Greener with you," said Ware's Kid. "Stick her back of the bar so's I can get her if there's call."

Hook-Hand again nodded approvingly. "An' is ut loaded?" he inquired.

"Nope. Aim to be *sure* about my shells. I'll load her when I take her."

"Oh, ho!" Hook-Hand's little eyes narrowed again. He nodded violently. "Sure, it's in me mind that the b'y has seen some av the trials and tribulations av this wicked wurrld. An' seen 'em through the smoke."

"Why"—Ware's Kid replied very solemnly—"it would mess up other business I've got right smart . . . staying in Las Tunas permanent."

Darkness had come, and the kerosene lamps were lit. More and more people appeared upon the sidewalks. Ware's Kid had no means of knowing for what hour the shooting up of the town was scheduled, but it seemed to him that right now was the proper time to begin what he termed, mentally, his night herding. He went back down East Street and turned wide around the corner of North Street. Already crowds stood along the Criterion's bar and about the games in the great adjoining room. He did not go in, but continued along North Street until he was opposite Williams's great Gem Variety Theater that marked the end of the lighted section of town.

As he stood there in the shadows beneath the wooden awning of a shabby saloon, Ware's Kid became conscious of droning voices from within the place. Evidently this saloon was not much patronized; the dingy front wore an apathetic resignation to neglect. He went softly to the door and peered around the jamb. Two old men stood midway down the bar with untouched drinks before them. Another leather-faced oldster with patriarchal white beard was behind the bar. The shorter of the drinkers was in the middle of an account of an Indian fight when Ware's Kid came in.

"Howdy," he said. "Ranger. Riding herd tonight."

"Howdy," nodded the old bartender.

But there was no friendliness in his face. The two old men opposite him also stared calculatingly at the smallish figure in Mexican clothing. They seemed to be weighing him, without being particularly impressed in his favor. Ware's Kid regarded the three of them with a slow turn of the head, gray-green eyes turning frosty, with that odd, electric glow shining far back. He waited, but they merely eyed him steadily.

"*Was* going to cache this Greener with you," he drawled. "But. . . ."

Eloquently he spat and was turning back to the door when the voice of Curran, the hardware man, sounded behind him. "The boy's all right, Jim Briggs! Don't you old mountain cats be combing him. I reckon all of you have heard of Bill Ware? Well. . . ."

Old Jim Briggs leaned suddenly across the bar and stared into the ranger's face. "Bill Ware's kid?" he cried. "Him as downed Black Alec Rawles? Son, I knowed yo' pappy thirty year back, an' I've heered a deal about his kid. If there's anything in this yere place ye want . . . just take her." He thrust out a gnarled paw, beaming.

Ware's Kid shook hands, then laid the shotgun upon the

bar. "Keep 'er handy," he requested. "Now, I got to ride herd some."

"Just a minute, Ware," said Curran, and Ware's Kid turned back to where the quartet were grouped together, whispering.

Old Jim Briggs had brought up three shotguns from beneath the bar and was scooping up double handfuls of shells to lay beside them.

"We're sort of old and puny," drawled Curran, "but if any shooting starts tonight, I reckon the four of us'll get a little lunch while the Williams crowd is having a full meal." And, while Ware's Kid watched with shadowy, grateful smile, the hardware man hauled up, from where it had hung inside his pants leg on a rawhide thong, a sawed-off shotgun. "I never could hit a barn a-wing with a Colt," confessed Curran, "but any damn' fool can shoot this thing."

"Thanks a heap," nodded the ranger, then went out.

As he made his second patrol of the lighted section of town, Ware's Kid fancied that a certain indefinable tension was present in the bearing, the expression of those he met. But as he went briskly along, glancing in at the Criterion, then turning up East Street, none made any hostile move, nor did he see Louis Sanders anywhere.

Now soft hurrying footsteps sounded behind him. He turned—to face that Mexican youth he had saved from Louis Sanders's quirt.

"¿Señor?" whispered the boy. "There is much talk in the town tonight. In the Three Jacks Saloon, friend of that *diablo,* Sanders, threaten to kill you . . . the bartender. He vows that no accursed ranger can put shame upon a friend of his and live. He has said that he will kill you upon sight. And he is *un hombre malo!* In his time in Las Tunas, he has already slain two men."

"Gracias," nodded Ware's Kid. "I shall not forget your friendly warning."

He walked on until he was out of the brightly lit part of the street, then slid noiselessly forward a few paces, and halted with back to a blank adobe wall in deep shadow. As he stood, staring up and down, he bethought him of the two Colts that hung, butts front, beneath his arms. He tried the cross-arm draw a few times and found it very simple. The guns came out flashingly.

Almost across from where he lurked was the Three Jacks Saloon. He walked over and went inside, wondering if he would find Louis Sanders here. But the ex-marshal was not among the dozen or more roughly dressed, hard-faced men who were drinking noisily, served by a rat-faced little bartender. Silence fell with his entrance; quite openly the patrons of the Three Jacks glowered at the ranger. He bore himself precisely as if the bar were deserted.

The bartender—evidently the man of whom the Mexican boy had spoken—came up to the bar like a cat and stood staring straight into the eyes of the ranger.

"Sarsaparilla," drawled Ware's Kid.

"So you come here, did you?" said the bartender in a low voice.

Ware's Kid eyed him thoughtfully, and the bartender returned his gaze without the slightest wavering of his own.

"So you come here, did you?" he repeated. "You think, mebbe, that you're goin' to git away with the bluff, do you?"

There was that about his tense posture, but most of all about his eyes, which assured Ware's Kid that he faced now a real killer and one on the verge of a killing. But, for all that he was tense as a coiled spring, he merely watched the bartender with deceptive quiet.

A sudden wave of blood flushed the sallow face, then the

bartender's right hand—that had all this time been concealed behind the bar—flashed into sight, bringing up a shiny revolver. But swiftly as it came, the ranger's left hand moved more rapidly still. The weapon was of the type usually scorned in the cow country—a stubby "center-break" double-action. Ware's Kid seized it; thumb and forefinger lifted the releasing lever; the heel of his palm depressed the barrel; it broke on its hinge and snapped shells back against the bartender's front. Then Ware's Kid had the revolver and was gripping the bartender by the collar. Holding the little weapon like a club, he smashed it into the bartender's temple, then dropped it as he let the senseless figure slide down behind the bar. He jerked one of his Colts and with it he menaced the astonished drinkers. For a minute he stared them down, then backed toward the door. Here he halted for an instant.

"Tell him"—he jerked his head toward the spot where the bartender lay—"if he's in town tomorrow, he'll sure stay . . . real permanent!"

He left that neighborhood swiftly, whirled down a cross street, and ducked into an alley, stepping out again upon East Street a block farther on. He stood for an instant upon the sidewalk, then went quickly inside the nearest saloon and out the back door, to move rapidly along the alley of that block. Near its end he entered the rear door of a saloon, went straight through it, out the front door, and crossed the street to repeat the maneuver on that side.

In fifteen minutes the town saw him ten times. He was here and there, appearing so noiselessly, vanishing so instantly, that men began to keep a sort of nervous watch for him. At last, as he stood flattened against the wall in a dark alley mouth, two men stopped on the lighted sidewalk almost within arm's length.

"Where's that damn' ranger?" one asked the other nervously.

"Damn' if I know," answered the other. "But I know I seen him five times in the last four minutes . . . an' I ain't had nine drinks tonight."

"Same here," snarled the first one. "My Gawd! You might think he was triplets or somethin'."

Ware's Kid grinned. Then suddenly he stiffened.

"Believe the boys is ready to start," snapped one of the men. They whirled and ran down North Street toward the Gem Variety Theater.

Ware's Kid listened. At first there was but the usual clamor of that noisy street. Then came a dull undertone that swelled and swelled. It was the voice of a mob—but a mob, he sensed, that was mechanically working itself into a fury. He knew that, once under way, mere momentum would carry it far. It must be checked in its beginning, else the sun would rise upon a town half destroyed, upon dead men.

Cautiously he peered out around the building-corner. Before the Gem, a few doors down the street, it seemed that North Street was filled from wall to wall. He whirled and sprinted down the alley, circled the block behind the Gem, crossed North Street well in the crowd's rear, and so came to the back door of Jim Briggs's saloon. Briggs, with Curran and the two other old men, was peering cautiously out the front door. At the scuff of feet they whirled like cats, and the gaping muzzles of four sawed-off shotguns covered Ware's Kid.

"Give me my Greener," he panted. Then, without waiting, he laid a hand upon the bar, vaulted over, scooped up the shotgun, and came into the center of the barroom again in the same manner. He broke the gun and jammed in two shells.

"Where yuh goin'?" demanded Curran, checking with

steely fingers the ranger's rush through the front door.

"Going to start 'em milling before they stampede," said Ware's Kid grimly, but with that cool light in his gray-green eyes.

"Reckon we'll trail along," said Curran, and Jim Briggs nodded.

The yelling mob, listening to two or three ringleaders, failed to observe the quintet that scattered to strategic points along its line, until Ware's Kid—with shotgun weaving deliberately in a wide arc that menaced many men—lifted his voice in a terrific yell. Instant silence fell. They whirled to face the small figure that grinned at them terribly.

" 'Twas all a mistake!" shouted Ware's Kid. "There won't *be* any riot!"

They gaped at him, robbed of initiative by his audacity, sure that, somehow, he concealed a trick. He had them checked, he knew, but he must start them moving in the way he intended before they recovered. The leaders had melted into the crowd somehow. Then suddenly came the voice of Louis Sanders.

"Yuh goin' to let one kid bluff yuh? Kill him an' let's go!"

But instantly, from another angle, came a voice that made either the ranger's or Louis Sanders's seem childish. "Shut up!" it commanded.

It was Jim Briggs, and sight of his weaving shotgun confirmed the crowd's belief in a trick. Curran and the other shotgun bearers, sensing the psychological effect to be gained, each with a whoop called attention to himself.

"Now, scatter!" barked Ware's Kid suddenly. "And *stay* scattered! Don't you go ganging up again anywheres tonight. There's heaps more'n us in this town!" He waved expansively at the second story windows that loomed darkly mysterious above the street. "Get and stay got!"

There was an instant's hesitancy, a tiny space of complete silence while the crowd searched for the faces—waited for the command—of its leaders, and in that silence, from five sides, sounded metallic clicks as the hammers trembled upon sawed-off shotguns.

Slowly the crowd began to mill. Ware's Kid, standing in the center of the street, moved swiftly backward and let them by. Men poured past him nervously, but at each doorway the crowd diminished. In ninety seconds, there were not upon that particular block the numbers that ordinarily it would have held at noontime.

"They're licked," declared Curran, as the four of them gathered in Jim Briggs's bar. "You couldn't get 'em together again with a broom. They figure there's a young army watching 'em. Tomorrow night . . . well, maybe it'll be to do all over again."

"Tomorrow night," grunted Ware's Kid, picking up his glass, "it'll be the new marshal's job. How!" He drained the glass ceremoniously. "Well," he said, "better show myself around some more. I'm real obliged to you-all. Hadn't helped me out, the way you did, never could've pulled that off."

"Shore," grinned Curran, " 'twas nothin'."

Ware's Kid had never been inside either the Gem or the Criterion. Outside Jim Briggs's place he stopped for a moment to listen to the voices of the Gem, then satisfied that it was noisy now but not menacing, he went up North Street to the great saloon and gambling hall of Joe Billings. The Criterion consisted of two huge rooms separated by a thin partition. One was the saloon, the other the gambling room. The private card rooms, Ware's Kid knew, were upstairs.

At the Criterion's bar, drinking, were not only the sporting crowd—although there were more of these than would be found in Hook-Hand Terry's Congress—but respectable citizens. As he came down the barroom many of the latter nodded cordially. Apparently word had spread of the quelling of the riot. He refused, with headshakes, offers of a dozen drinks and moved over to the great gilded archway that led into the gambling room.

There was a tense sort of order prevailing among the groups around the several games, and, satisfied with his inspection, he was about to turn back toward the bar when he heard a sort of snarl behind him and a scuffing of many feet at the bar—which he recognized instantly as the movement of men to right and left, out of range.

"So there yuh are!" snarled Louis Sanders.

Ware's Kid, cursing mentally that he had been surprised by the man he had been hunting, turned very slowly. Evidently Sanders had been drinking. His face, marked by Ware's fists, was darkly flushed. He stood with feet somewhat apart, leaning a little forward. The quirt looped to his left hand—which he seemed never to discard—was *lap-lapping* his boot toe. The tiny red veins were swollen around his eyes. His teeth showed beneath the long, black mustache. He was in a killing humor, no doubt of that, and his hand was upon the white butt of his Colt. Ware's Kid surveyed him blankly from beneath drooping lids.

"So yuh're goin' to kill me on sight, are yuh?" cried Sanders, and Ware's Kid had to admire the man for pausing, at a moment like this, to build up some slight justification for a killing.

"Who told you-all that?" he drawled curiously.

"Yuh can't fool me that way," roared Sanders, and Ware's Kid saw his big fingers quivering above the Colt's butt. He knew the signs. "Don't yuh pull a gun on me! Don't yuh pull that gun!" cried Sanders.

"Ain't pulling a gun." Ware's Kid lifted his hands so that they were palm outward before his breast. Steadily he stared into the red-veined eyes of the ex-marshal—and folded his arms. "But turn loose your six-shooter, or I'll down you."

Sanders's fingers closed hard upon the butt of his Colt. But as it lifted a little from the holster, Ware's Kid jerked both his pistols.

Sanders, as Dave Barrow had warned Ware, was something of a gunman himself. He had drawn the white-handled Colt from the holster, and only by the thinnest of margins did Ware's Kid flip back the hammer first.

Men, watching from the rear, saw the thumb of Sanders's gun hand, the thumb that was crooked to jerk back the hammer, torn abruptly from the hand by a bullet. Saw Sanders throw the gun into his left hand with the flashing border shift. But by that time Ware's Kid had fired three times more, and Sanders's bullet went wild.

The ex-marshal crashed face downward on the floor.

As Ware's Kid leaned forward with Colts covering the still figure, a pistol shot sounded from the rear of the room. There was a metallic *clang,* and Ware staggered. Then he recovered himself, whirled upon a heel, and sent five bullets at a squat, sandy-haired man who stood almost against the rear wall with smoking six-shooter in his hand. As the pungent smoke wreathed slowly up toward the great cut-glass chandeliers, the squat man sagged to the floor and lay still.

In the silence of the great barroom sounded now a single, muffled thud. Ware's Kid, whose nerves were on edge, whirled like a cat in the direction of the sound, with both Colts at hip level.

"Don't worry, Ware," Dave Barrow's piping tenor counseled him. "I laid this 'n' out myself. He was fixin' to take a shot at you."

Ware's Kid nodded, but almost absently. He stood in the barroom's center with eyes shuttling from the body of the squat, sandy-haired man against the far wall to that of Louis Sanders. Suddenly he stooped beside the latter.

Sanders lay with arms outflung, the heavy quirt, still looped to his left hand, curling around the arm like a dead snake. Very deliberately, Ware's Kid began to roll Sanders's coat sleeves to the elbow. When he had finished, he stood up, and all in the barroom and in the packed doorway of the gambling room were staring. He motioned toward Sanders.

"Know him?" he demanded.

There was an instant of puzzlement, then they answered him with a sudden amazed roar.

"Red Sleeves!"

For from elbow to wrist Sanders's arms were covered with the red flannel of his shirt sleeves.

"I come down from Las Tunas way a-lookin' for him. Thought maybe he'd hunt cover in a crowd. Figured, too, he'd be about ready to start on another job. Remember, all his jobs were about three months apart. I was lookin' for a man with a scar in his left palm. In four, five robberies they found in the dust, where the gang had squatted waiting for the stage, a left hand print with a scar across it. Today, I knocked this fella down. Later on, happened to notice the print of his left hand makes a mark mighty like a scar . . . good enough to fool a body. And I reckon carrying that quirt was a strong habit of Sanders."

"Nobody ever saw him without it," nodded Dave Barrow. "But these two fellows here?"

"His gang," grunted Ware's Kid. "If I'm not mistaken."

"We can mighty soon find out!"

This was Curran, the hardware man, who shoved through the crowd to the side of Dave Barrow with small eyes twinkling, took a glass of whiskey from the bar, forced open the mouth of his victim, and poured the liquor down.

The man, a tow-haired, furtive-faced individual, coughed violently. His eyes opened, and after a moment he sat up—to behold Curran, ferociously grim of expression, bearing down upon him with a suggestively dangling noose. The prisoner scrambled to his feet, but Dave Barrow gripped his arm and held him as if he had been a child. Curran stopped and turned to the tense watchers as for final affirmation.

"Then you're all agreed that he is Red Sleeves? And that there's no use bothering to wait, since he's been tried fair and square?"

A rumbling murmur of assent answered him.

The prisoner gaped fearfully at the sinister noose. "Red Sleeves!" he cried shrilly. "Hell! *I* ain't Red Sleeves! That was Sanders. Oh, I admit I rode with him, but 'twas 'cause I was skeered not to! You wouldn't hang me! I'll tell you all about it! But don't hang me, gentlemen! For God's sake. . . ."

"And that," grinned Curran, "is that."

The doorway of Dave Barrow's store was rather well-filled in the hour of early morning coolness. Curran and Dave Barrow, with a waspish-looking little man between them, were glancing with vast satisfaction up and down the pleasingly unmarred lines of buildings on North Street.

"Well, there goes Ware's Kid," remarked Park Cheyne, the waspish-looking one.

He polished the star upon his vest with a cuff and stared absently after the diminishing horseman, who was now well out on the trail to the ranger's camp.

"Call him by his own name," growled old Curran, turning quickly upon the new marshal of Las Tunas. "That's Stephen Ware . . . Texas Ranger. He can stand on his own legs. He don't have to get by on account of being somebody's kid. No, sir! He's an uncombed flash of lightning with a big slab of rock for a backbone and a barb-wire fence all around. Call him by his name as you'd call any other man."

The Trail of a Fool

Stephen Ware—who had upon a time, both in the rangers and outside, been known as "Ware's Kid"—found Cholla rather more than normally active by the standards of a Southwestern cowtown in late afternoon. Up and down the single sandy street the hitch racks before the several saloons were nearly hidden from view by tethered cow ponies. He reined in Rocket, his big black stallion, midway between the ends of the twin rows of low adobes that constituted the place and slouched comfortably in the saddle to study the fronts of saloons, stores, and eating houses with thoughtful gray-green eyes. Crudely printed posters upon diverse house walls informed him that the reason for the activity he noted was an election.

It seemed to him that, if those horse thieves from Tornillo way made Cholla their headquarters, he was as likely to stumble upon some trace of them in one place as another. He had nothing more to go upon, in seeking them now in Cholla, than the word of that youthful Mexican sheepherder he had met two days before. This youngster—with whom the ranger had shared a meal—had let slip a remark concerning a certain quintet of horsemen who had passed him as he herded his master's sheep.

"So they moved with this *manada* to the west, *señor,* toward Cholla. I suppose that to the ranches up there they sell their horses, then, in Cholla, spend the money. Ah! It must be a pleasant life, that of. . . ."

Then, suddenly, he had seemed to become afraid. No

prompting—and Ware spoke Spanish as fluently as English—
had served to extract from him more than mumbled protests
that he knew nothing, nothing at all. Little enough, in a way,
but it was all that Ware had to go on. He had been ordered by
the captain of his company to go into the Tornillo country,
where much fine saddle stock had been disappearing mysteriously. He had been told only to stop the stealing. Of the identity of the thieves, or their method of operation, he had been
told nothing—for nothing, it seemed, was known.

From the Palace Saloon, directly across from where he
had halted the stallion, now came the muffled voices of a
number of men, with, as overtone, the asthmatic squeal of an
ancient accordion. Ware touched Rocket with a spur, then
kneed the stallion across to the Palace's hitch rack. He
slipped down—a smallish figure, eighteen or nineteen at
most, who rode as if he and the great stallion were one—
pulled the split reins of the Mexican bridle over the big
black's head, and twisted them deftly in a looped half-hitch
over the rail. Rocket nuzzled his rider's shoulder, and Ware,
from a pocket of his embroidered Mexican jacket, drew a
leathery tortilla and fed it to the stallion. Then he turned and
clicked across the board-floored verandah of the saloon with
the stiff-legged gait of the horseman-born.

In the doorway he halted, as any wise man would have
done in that day and place, to stare up and down the long,
smoke-wreathed, noisy room. Here, too, he saw crudely
printed election posters upon the plastered walls. Obviously
there were men from several outfits at the long bar. This was
apparent by the way they gathered unconsciously in little
knots about their drinks. Several youngsters were jigging in
the corner to the left of the door, around an ancient Negro
who, with swaying, gray-wooled head, pumped frantically at
his accordion.

Ware edged in between two of the groups and ordered a drink. Those who chanced to see him enter stared curiously at the Mexican finery, at the bronzed, expressionless face, the inscrutable gray-green eyes that were shaded by the wide brim of bullion-ornamented sombrero. They noted the absence of any visible weapons, for he had left the little Winchester carbine in its saddle scabbard. Apparently he did not mark the attention he had drawn. He tossed down his drink, then half turned with left elbow upon the bar to make aimless circles with empty glasses while he seemed to watch the dancers about the Negro musician.

He was by no means trying to pick his horse thieves from this crowd. He knew far too well that, if and when he identified them, they would be no different in appearance from any other cowboy. Rather, he sought for some incident which might lead to evidence. His successes in the past, the successes that had given him a reputation, had come to him usually in a way that seemed to the casual observer accidental. Actually, he had discovered the man he wanted because of his trick of being ever patiently on the alert for some tiny happening that, properly considered and followed up, was like a door opening. So now he leaned easily against the bar, confident that, if he but watched long enough and carefully enough, the men would reveal themselves somehow.

There was one cowboy upon the edge of the jigging group who watched the ranger furtively. He was not dancing, this stocky, yellow-haired, round-faced youth. Ware noted him, for there was that about the cowboy which would lead men to pass him over unconsciously, a certain insignificance that was as apparent as a label. But, staring absently at the dancers, Ware stared directly past the cowboy, and apparently the youngster believed himself to be the target of that inscrutable regard. He kept turning, apparently without seeing the motionless figure up the bar, glancing toward the saloon door as if expecting someone to enter, but each time eyeing Ware. At last he seemed to grow uncomfortable and at the same time emboldened by Ware's quiet, for he whirled and glared at the ranger. They were perhaps twenty feet apart when for the first time their eyes met squarely.

"Well!" snarled the cowboy. "Reckon yuh'll know me ag'in?"

Ware made no reply. This sudden thrusting into his attention of a heretofore almost unnoticed figure somewhat surprised him, but he evinced his feeling by no alteration of brown face, merely watched the cowboy levelly.

The latter's courage seemed to swell with the ranger's negligent attitude. He stood with hands on hips and glared furiously. Ware had an odd feeling that the fellow had recognized him as a ranger. This instinct was verified by the cowboy's next remark.

"Reckon yuh think just 'cause yuh're a ranger, yuh can come hellin' it around Cholla! Well, I'm tellin' yuh right now that. . . ."

"Shut up," snapped Ware abruptly.

Other sounds in the saloon had been hushed. In the silence the command had cracked like a whiplash. Men started involuntarily. The effect of the words upon the cowboy surprised all in the barroom—not excepting Ware—for the heavy Colt sagging at the fellow's right hip came flashingly into his hand.

He leaped straight at the still motionless ranger. Oddly, he seemed to forget to flip back the hammer, but instead jerked it aloft like a club. Men held their breath, finding no sign of a weapon about the ranger. But Ware's amazement held him still only for the barest fraction of an instant, then—not for nothing had he practiced for weary hours at getting out his twin white-handled Colts from the concealed John Wesley Hardin holsters—his right hand slid beneath his jumper with the smooth speed of a snake disappearing into a hole and then reappeared with a continuation of the same movement—Colt-armed.

He fired once, then the cowboy had cannoned into him, knocking him sideways. His boot toe caught upon a projecting plank of the rough floor, and he went down. The cowboy stumbled, also, but did not fall, nor did he stop. Out through the door he went. Ware, rolling over, sent two bullets after him, but did no more than nick the door facing. He came to his feet like a cat, but already the doorway was jammed with men watching the fugitive's flight.

Before Ware could push through them, there sounded upon the street the beat of a horse's hoofs—of a horse rowelled into a racing gallop. At the sound, Ware shrugged and reholstered his Colt. After all, he had no particular reason to chase that fool unless, perhaps, to discover the reason for his sudden panic.

For there was no doubt in Ware's mind, now that he had had opportunity to consider the distorted face of the cowboy as he had leaped forward, the fellow had been moved by nothing but overpowering panic. Then with those in the doorway he moved outside to stare up and down the street. Already the rolling dust cloud was far away. A tiny grin lifted one corner of his thin mouth. The fellow, he thought, had a good horse. Unconsciously he glanced toward the end of the hitch rack, and his face twisted in sudden fury. For Rocket, the black stallion—his beloved Rocket—was gone!

Ware whirled. A knot of cowboys were staring at him. "Sheriff?" he rasped. "Marshal? Hell! Anybody with a badge?"

They eyed him curiously for an instant, then one jerked a thumb vaguely over his shoulder. "This is election day," he grinned. "Jim Weatherbee's sheriff now, but Tom White may be sheriff tomorrow."

"Where's Weatherbee?"

A thick-set man with brown, short-nosed, big-chinned face came down the street at this moment. He was amazingly bowed of leg, and he toed in peculiarly with his right foot, the result of a fall beneath a stumbling horse. Upon his ancient, flapping vest was a small gold star.

"That's Weatherbee," the cowpuncher told Ware.

The sheriff, after a hard stare at Ware and a nod for the cowboys, would have gone on into the Palace, but Ware moved into his path.

"Fellow stole my stallion," he stated, then waited.

"Stole your stallion?" repeated Weatherbee blankly.

The cowboys, too, seemed surprised. Apparently they had taken it for granted that the departing one had gone upon his own mount.

"Who was it?" snapped the sheriff.

"That fella, Curly," said the cowboy who had been doing the talking. " 'Twas in the Palace. Curly starts a riot with this fella, jerks a gun, and rushes like he aims to pistol-whip him, then this fella draws. Shoots an' misses. Curly, he rams into him, knocks him over, an' just keeps on goin'."

"Want a horse," snapped Ware. "Goin' to get Mister Curly. Get him if I have to follow him the rest of my life."

"Now calm down, young fella," advised the sheriff. "I'm takin' keer o' things in this county. If somebody steals a hoss in Cholla, that's for me to handle. But they's somethin' funny about all this. How come Curly, he tangled with you?"

"Oh, hell!" exploded Ware, finding fluency in his rage. "Goin' to talk me to death? This Curly stole my stallion . . .

best horse in Texas. Done gone ten minutes now. Going to stand here gassing till he's gone a week? I'm not asking help from you. I'm asking where can I get a horse. Best 'n' in town. Want to buy him. Give twice what he's worth."

"Look here, young fella," exploded the sheriff. I ain't a-takin' nothin' off smart alecks. When I ask questions around here, I aim to git an answer."

"Oh, hell!" cried Ware. "He's started again. Can't anybody in this town talk sense?"

The sheriff's bulldog face was reddened with injured dignity. He had taken a half step toward Ware when from the door of the Palace came a big, capable-looking ranchman. "Wait a minute, Weatherbee," said the big man calmly. "This boy's lost a pet hoss, an' yuh can't hardly blame him fer bein' sore about it. Nat'rally he wants to be chasin' Curly, 'stead o' standin' here talkin' while Curly gits clean away."

"But I want to know . . . ," insisted the sheriff stubbornly.

"Now, now," smiled the big man. "The boy's right. There's been a whole lot o' talkin' done, when ridin's the thing that gits a hoss thief. Who might yuh-all be, son?"

"Ranger. Think this Curly knew it, too. Can *you* tell me where I can buy a horse . . . a good horse?"

"Don't know about buyin' one," drawled the big man. "But I might loan yuh one. Tell you what, Weatherbee . . . I'll put this boy ab'd my foreman's hoss, an' trail along with him. Mebbe we'll catch up with Mister Curly."

"Not unless Rocket busts his leg," sneered Ware. "Isn't a horse in this neck of the woods can touch the poorest colt ever foaled out of a Swayn mare."

"Oh, ho," nodded the big man curiously. "So that's a Swayn stallion yuh lost. Don't blame yuh fer r'arin' back." Then his blue eyes narrowed suddenly. "Yo' name happen to be Ware?"

125

Impatiently Ware nodded, and the big man thrust out his hand swiftly.

"My name's Boggs," he volunteered, "an' I'm sure glad to meet yuh! We've heard about yuh-all. Now, come on! That bay there's my foreman's hoss. Take it an' welcome."

Ware waited for no further invitation. He jerked the reins loose and threw them over the bay's head with a flashing, critical glance at the animal. It was a half-blood and a fine horse, but by comparison with the vanished Rocket. . . .

Boggs, too, had mounted. His animal was a tall, rawboned gray. He whirled it deftly and rode back to where the puzzle-faced sheriff waited.

"Now, don't yuh-all steal that election, Weatherbee," he grinned. "Give Tom White an even show, 'cause the people's will must be obeyed."

Ware, spurring the bay in the direction the fugitive Curly had taken, found his lead easily cut down by Boggs's ugly gray. The ranchman's eyes twinkled as he came alongside the ranger.

"Ain't disputin' what yuh said about the stallion," he shouted above the thud of pounding hoofs, "but, if we git back yo' Rocket, I'd shore admire to run Major, here, ag'in' him."

The trail of Rocket, the black stallion, was clear in the sand. For a mile beyond the outskirts of Cholla they followed it easily; then the sand thinned, giving way to barely covered rock. Boggs nodded.

"It'll be hard, now," he shouted in Ware's ear. "This patch o' rocky ground's pretty big. Even an Indian couldn't keep a trail up here."

And so it proved. The trail died abruptly, and, circle as they would, they found no trace of hoof prints. Ware reined in the bay and stared glumly at Boggs. The ranchman crooked a leg comfortably about his saddle horn and built a cigarette, whistling soundlessly beneath his breath.

"What's beyond?" asked Ware.

"Well, sort o' depends on the direction," shrugged Boggs. "West o' here's Scalp Creek, an' farther west are the Emigrant Mountains. T'other side the mountains there's *malpais* for a long way, then there's some scattered ranches . . . the Crowfoot outfit an' a few others."

"What's north of Cholla?"

"Arrowhead outfit, an' farther south the Three Prod. My outfit, the Lazy D, is quite a way east o' town. Here!"

From a saddlebag he drew a folded newspaper and flattened it upon his knee. With the lead of a cartridge from his belt he outlined very roughly the lay-out of the region. Ware studied the map thoughtfully, then sat for minutes staring vacantly straight ahead.

"East of the Lazy D," he asked abruptly, "what's up that way?"

"Nothin' fer a long way. Mighty pore country."

"Curly came in with that last bunch of horses from Tornillo, didn't he?"

Then, as Boggs hesitated, with blue eyes narrowing, calculating, Ware grinned slightly.

"Yeah, I thought he did! How many of those horses did you buy, Boggs?"

Boggs still eyed him thoughtfully. At last a twinkle crept into his blue eyes. "Am I . . . uh . . . talkin' in court-like?" he inquired blandly.

Ware grinned back at him with equal frankness. "Why, I reckon," he drawled, "I aim to get the horse thieves this trip, rather'n the horses."

"A'right, then! Curly come up with the last bunch, like yuh said. About sixty head o' good stock, they brought. Me an' Jack Lowry o' the Arrowhead an' Wiggins o' the Three Prod, we split 'em about even. Them hosses was right foot-sore, so we bought 'em pretty cheap."

"Where'd the fellows go?"

"Don't know," shrugged Boggs. "Curly, he stuck in Cholla. Others rode on north, I reckon. That was four, five days ago."

Again Ware studied the crude map. "Lazy D a horse ranch?" he inquired briefly.

"Why, pretty much," said Boggs. "So's the Arrowhead an' the Three Prod, as far as that goes, though Wiggins, he runs right smart o' cows, too."

"How many of your men in town today?"

"Today's election day," Boggs reminded him. "Tom White, he's put up consid'able battle ag'in' Weatherbee. Country's all het up about it, so all the boys, barrin' just a hand or two on each ranch, is likely in Cholla today."

"When's the election over? When'll they be going on?"

"Not until day after tomorrow sometime. The winner . . . Weatherbee or White . . . will throw a big dance tomorrow night, an' I reckon it'll be around noon the day after before some o' the boys'll be fit to fork a bronc'."

Slowly Ware shook his head. "Well," he drawled, "I've ridden some, seen right smart of country, considerable folks, but you-all Cholla people are about the easiest passel of nit-wits I ever came up against. Come on, let's travel to the Lazy D."

"What's the big idee?" demanded Boggs, spurring his gray after Ware.

"Mister," said Ware, "when you take a look at your horse pasture and see the place where your horse band used to be, you'll sure *sabe* a heap."

Boggs gaped at him, but Ware set a pace so fast through

the brush that conversation was impossible for a couple of miles. Actually Ware was furious. If what he believed were true, he had no more than an outside chance to recover Rocket. After a while he slackened the gait a little so that Boggs could ride stirrup to stirrup with him.

The big ranchman's face was a study in mixed emotions, but now there was, chiefly, an odd expectancy in his expression, as if he waited for the younger man to take the initiative.

"I'm not sympathizing with you-all any," said Ware at last. "You ought to know a dog that brings a bone'll carry a bone. You-all never got too curious about those horses coming from the south. Well, the map you drew back there tells the whole story. Tornillo country's getting too hot for this gang. They figure . . ."—he turned suddenly sideways in the saddle to glare at Boggs—"who was leading this outfit?"

"Fella named Acree," replied Boggs meekly. "But I 'low mebbe 'tweren't his real name."

"You're learning," Ware complimented him sourly. "How'd he look?"

"Little, dark-complected, good-lookin' hairpin."

"Left-handed?"

"Uhn-huh! Uhn-huh! Packed a Forty-Four Colt on the right side, butt front."

"Skeets Winder. Wanted in Goliad County for murder. Five hundred dollars reward."

"Yuh was sayin' *they* figgered?" prompted Boggs.

"They figured 'twas time to move on. They brought this last bunch of stuff north and unloaded on you-all. They knew about election day. Figured to clean up the Lazy D, the Arrowhead, and the Three Prod, then cross the Emigrants to the northwest and come out on the railroad somewheres."

"The hell!" snarled Boggs.

It spoke much for both Ware's reputation and his person-

129

ality that this big, capable ranchman accepted his deductions at face value. Boggs spurred the gray on as if he could not reach the Lazy D quickly enough. The bay could not keep up. At last Ware hailed Boggs, and the ranchman slowed, if impatiently, until the ranger could overtake him.

"Here's the way I figure," remarked Ware. "They'll clean out the Lazy D first. It's farthest from the way they're going to head. That'll leave 'em the Three Prod and the Arrowhead. Both outfits are on the trail they'll naturally follow toward Scalp Creek and the Emigrants. Question is, which of the two would they make for first . . . that is, if we don't find 'em at the Lazy D? . . . I figure we're too late for that. Arrowhead's closer to town. Reckon they'd go in there first, then clean out the Three Prod?"

Boggs considered. "If she's like yuh think," he said slowly, "they got ever'thing figgered out to a gnat's hair. Chances are, one o' the bunch, anyhow, knows this country. So they'd know the only pass in the Emigrants around Cholla is due west o' the Arrowhead. So, they'd clean up the Three Prod first, after leavin' my place."

"How far do we have to ride to know about your horse band?" inquired Ware frowningly.

"Four, five miles yet. I got me a line camp between the ranch house an' town. Ought to be one man there."

Actually they knew almost beyond a doubt that it was as Ware had believed, well before they reached the adobe shack that served as a line camp. They ran into the trail of a big horse band, a fresh trail, pointing somewhat north of west. Boggs swore bitterly and pushed on.

"If they've hurt Bill Roberts . . . ," he gritted.

They found the Lazy D man just outside the adobe house. He was fairly riddled with bullets. On the ground before him was a six-shooter, lying where it had fallen from his dead fingers. Evidently he had been approached by men who did not alarm him; perhaps he had pulled his gun only after bullets had thudded into his own body. Ware picked up the Colt and turned the cylinder. Only two shells had been fired. He turned to Boggs, who was kneeling beside the dead man.

"How many you reckon are in this gang?"

"Four. Five, if Curly's caught up with 'em."

Ware nodded and looked swiftly about him. The open door of the adobe attracted him. He went inside the house and came out with an expression of satisfaction, bearing a Winchester carbine and a box of .44s. On the foreman's saddle had been no rifle.

"Ready?" he asked Boggs.

Boggs stared at him for a long half minute, then nodded. "Young fella, I shore like yo' style," he said simply. "Five to two. Huh! Them fellows is shore goin' to hub hell!"

An odd, electric glint showed in Ware's gray-green eyes, but, when he answered the rancher, his tone was merely conversational. "They're going to see some misery and see her through the smoke," he nodded.

They followed the wide trail of the horse band. Ware took the lead now, motioning Boggs to keep half a head behind him. Finally, well beyond that point where, riding toward the line camp, they had first seen the trail, Ware grunted in a savage sort of satisfaction. Boggs, staring in the direction indicated by Ware's forefinger, nodded quickly. It was a tiny patch of red in the dust. Ware leaned far out of the saddle and swept his fingers through the spot, studied the smear upon them.

"Blood, all right."

A couple of miles farther on they found a man lying in the greasewood to the right of the trail. They approached him cautiously, although he did not seem to hear the pound of the

131

galloping hoofs. Ware's gun flashed into his hand. He slipped from the saddle and ran swiftly up to the prostrate figure and twitched the heavy six-shooter from the horse thief's holster. Then, only, did the man's eyes open feebly, and but for a moment. The front of his flannel shirt was caked with blood. Boggs swung down with face like brown granite, blue eyes icy, tense hand knotted around his Colt butt.

"Know 'im?" inquired Ware, staring down at the thin, brown face, now pallid with the death color.

"He was one of the gang. They called him Pete," said Boggs. "Bill Roberts shore buttonholed him."

Ware stripped back the shirt from the fellow's chest, stared for a moment at the gaping hole that welled blood, then rose. "Nothing to do for him," he shrugged. "Your man, Roberts, sure had a gun that shot where he held it. Let's go."

"They're headin' for the Three Prod, all right," said Boggs. "Three, four hours ahead, I figger. Now, there's no use our ridin' out there. Let's us cut out across an' bushwhack 'em on the trail between the Three Prod an' the Arrowhead."

Forthwith he whirled his gray due west. They pelted through greasewood and mesquite and cactus for miles. Even the range-bred animals were breathing heavily when, at last, they came to a trail, fairly well-defined, running roughly north and south. There were no traces of the horse band on this trail, and up it, toward the Three Prod, they rode until they came to the dry bed of an arroyo, across which the trail led.

"We'll wait here," said Boggs briefly.

The arroyo was nine or ten feet deep. The horses would not be visible to the oncoming thieves until they had ridden down into the very bed of the arroyo. So they swung down and squatted with backs against a wall to smoke and overhaul their weapons and wait. An hour passed draggingly. The sun was sweeping down the horizon toward the jagged blue peaks of the Emigrants. Shadows were lengthening. Frequently one or the other rose and lifted his bare head cautiously above the arroyo rim.

It was Boggs who, getting up to take a look, turned with grimly tightened mouth. "Comin'," he grunted. "Ready? Well, young fella, there's goin' to be some powder burned in a little. If . . . if it turns out that-a-way, why . . . so long."

Ware looked. Perhaps a mile to the northeast a cloud of dust was rising, slowly billowing up from the trail. He glanced calculatingly at the arroyo walls and nodded to himself. "Let's get aboard," he suggested. "Reckon you'll have to kind of scrooch down, Boggs, else you'll stick up over the edge, and they'll see you."

The pound of hoofs sounded louder and louder, a muffled drumming. Boggs on one side of the trail, Ware on the other, hugging close to the wall, they watched and waited tensely.

A lithe youngster of daredevil face popped down into the arroyo between them. Behind him came the van of stolen horses from the Three Prod and Lazy D. He shifted in the saddle, this one who rode point. As he turned, the loop of Ware's rope settled about his neck. He came from the saddle like a frog, with arms and legs waving wildly, a cry of alarm choking hoarsely in his throat.

The horse band milled for an instant, then shrill yells from the thieves behind drove them on, and they shot up the far side of the arroyo. The fellow whom Ware had roped came with a jerking of the rawhide lariat almost under the hoofs of Ware's bay. He struck squarely upon his head and lay still.

Ware stared down at him for an instant, then the sight of the unnaturally twisted head told him that this one's days of riding were over for always.

In the midst of the columns of horses now appeared another of the thieves, a tall, thin man wearing his left arm in a sling improvised from his neckerchief. He was staring sideways as he entered the arroyo, so he looked straight into the eyes of Boggs. He yelled shrilly, and his hand flashed to his hip. Boggs drove an accurate bullet through his face, and the next instant he was on the ground, under the hoofs of the herd.

Then both Boggs and Ware urged their mounts against the stream of horses pouring down into the arroyo. They feared that the man's yell and the sound of the shot had alarmed the other thieves. It took a minute or two—first to check the horses, then to push their way through them. When they reached the arroyo rim, they found their fears were justified.

Two horsemen were four or five hundred yards away, racing toward the distant Scalp Creek. The rider in the van was obviously Curly, for he bestrode Rocket, Ware's black stallion. The other, by a process of elimination, must be Skeets Winder.

The pursuers had the advantage of fresher horses—fresher for the hour's rest in the arroyo's bed. They sped after the thieves and very slowly cut down the others' lead. But cut it down they did, although still there was no possibility of shooting at them with any chance of accuracy.

They saw the horse thieves casting frequent glances at the back trail, over shoulders or from under their elbows, while inch by inch, almost, they crept up on Curly and Skeets Winder. But there was the great danger that, if the fugitives could maintain a lead of even a few hundred yards until darkness, in the broken foothills of the Emigrants, they might escape. Only the fact that Rocket had traveled that day more miles than the other three horses permitted them to keep within sight of him now.

Skeets Winder's mount began to lag; he was limping slightly. He was perhaps fifty yards behind Curly. Winder yelled shrilly, and Curly whirled, involuntarily slackened pace a trifle—enough to let Skeets Winder cut down the lead to thirty, twenty, fifteen yards.

Curly—poor, dumb Curly about whom hung that aura of insignificance, of futility—was doomed. Skeets Winder's hand leaped up. He fired twice, and again. Curly's body jerked in the saddle as if he had been struck with a club. He fell forward upon the horn.

A hand came up, as if in farewell to the world about him, a lovely land that swept away across miles and miles of pungent-smelling greasewood to the narrow stream of Scalp Creek and beyond to the heaved-up foothills of the Emigrants; a land bathed now in the deep, yellow sunlight of late afternoon, when already the mountains were taking on the purple haze of evening; a land that was full of peace and the promise of peace, but had no peace for him. He slipped sideways. The hand clawed at Rocket's mane for an instant, then he was upon the ground, and Skeets Winder, spurring alongside Rocket, changed mounts at a gallop, bent low over the saddle horn, and struck home the rowels.

Ware, sliding the bay to a stop, flung himself from the saddle and took two long running steps forward, then halted with rifle held loosely. He drew two deep, deliberate breaths, then slowly the rifle came up. The first bullet was a clean miss. He shifted aim slightly then. With the flat, vicious report of the second shot, Skeets Winder came from the saddle as if scooped out by an unseen hand. Rocket trotted on a few steps, then stopped. Ware yelled at him shrilly, and Rocket turned with ears pricked forward. When his master yelled a second time, he came trotting back.

★ ★ ★ ★ ★

"Funny thing about it," said Ware thoughtfully as they stood staring down into the face of Curly, "is this here poor nitwit. I figure they left him in town to kind of ride herd on things. When I walked into the Palace, he knew me for a ranger. I reckon I've got to quit wearing this Mexican outfit. It's getting me too well known. But if he hadn't gone and lost his head and stolen Rocket, chances are he wouldn't be lying here dead, and we wouldn't've cleaned up the Tornillo gang."

"She's shore a hard country on damn' fools," nodded Boggs. "Yes, suh! They ride a hard trail."

The Ranger Way

Leesville was but a huddle of low, dingy brown adobes—and not too large a huddle, for twelve or fourteen miles up the river, in a crow-flight, was Las Tunas, the real town of the region. But Leesville, with the wide, yellowish stretches of the range country behind it, served as a subordinate supply station to the cowmen and sheepmen and the small farmers, and so, with a couple of stores, three saloons, and several eating houses, justified its sleepy existence. Too, there was a little trading back and forth across the river with the people who lived in and around Concepción, the Mexican village that lay some five miles to the west of Leesville.

Ware jogged quietly into Leesville from Las Tunas and reined in Rocket before Paddy Larkin's saloon. Four or five indolent loungers on the saloon verandah watched him with a sort of lackluster curiosity. As he slipped to the ground and threw the reins over Rocket's head, they sized him up—a small, brown-faced youngster, certainly no more than twenty-one, with great, black, bullion-embroidered sombrero shading gray-green eyes, short jacket of tanned goatskin fringed to the elbow, and bell-bottomed Mexican trousers of fine blue woolen with rows of silver buttons bordering the crimson insert of their outer seams. The loungers noted also that he wore no visible weapon.

They saw him glance curiously up and down the short single street of Leesville and were interested to observe the Mexican, sauntering along the dusty street, stop short for an instant with sight of the stranger, then leap forward with much gesticulation and excited chattering, like one who discovers an old and dear friend. They watched the pair move up to the bench upon a deserted verandah and there sit for perhaps a quarter hour, engaged in earnest conversation. It being a lazy spring day, the loungers did not exert themselves too violently to speculate concerning this spectacle.

Presently Ware came clicking at his stiff-legged horseman's gait, back to Paddy Larkin's, nodded briefly to those upon the verandah, and went inside. Paddy himself was behind the bar, talking with—or, rather, listening to—a very tall, very lean individual who wore the wide Stetson, the buttonless vest over calico shirt, the overalls, and spurred boots of the cowboy, a dark-haired, black-eyed, grim-faced man who was engaged in a bitter tirade against something or other.

Ware's swift side-glance at this one left him vaguely puzzled. About the fellow's lean waist were crossed cartridge belts and low upon each hip sagged a heavy black-butted Colt; the toes of the holsters were secured by rawhide thongs to the man's boot-tops. Then a slight shift in the man's position revealed a star upon his vest. That explained the somewhat unusual armament.

Paddy waddled up the bar, set bottle and glass before Ware, remarked that it was a fine day, indeed, it was, then waddled back to the other customer, who had not turned his head toward Ware.

"That's whut I always said . . . ," the lean man took up his conversation again with Paddy Larkin. "They come into a town an' don't do more'n the peace off'cers. Then when the trouble's over, everybody says . . . the rangers done it! Well, all I got to say is, I saw considerable rangers in my time an', so fer as I can tell, ain't none of 'em got no more legs nor no more arms than I got, an' none I see is any better with a six-shooter or Winchester than I am. An' I ain't see none yit as'd go prancin' anywhere I'd be skeered to foller 'em. Trouble is, they got a name an' so they git credit fer doin' everything as happens within a mile of 'em. An' half the time it was somebody else as did the job."

Ware stared blankly before him at the back-bar. It was not the first time he had encountered such a feeling in a peace officer. Not that the feeling was widespread. Most city marshals, sheriffs, and their deputies were willing enough to accept Texas Ranger assistance when situations got out of hand, but always there would be the occasional exception who was unwilling to admit the need of the rangers or give them credit for performing the hard work the peace officers shirked.

The deputy's tirade continued. Ware finished his drink, walked down the bar, and laid two bits before Paddy Larkin.

"C'rect," nodded Paddy. "Come in ag'in."

"Thanks," said Ware.

"Just ridin' through?" inquired Paddy sociably.

Ware nodded. "Riding through. You see . . . I'm a ranger."

At which the man with the star turned slowly. His hard, black eyes studied Ware intently. Ware met his regard steadily for a moment. He saw that the star was that of a deputy sheriff.

"Talk to you?" Ware inquired.

After another instant of staring, the deputy nodded slowly. Ware gave him credit for seeming in no wise confused at having had his indictment of the rangers heard by one of the force. He admitted, too, that this lean, two-gunned figure was a capable-looking individual.

He jerked his head toward the saloon door and moved that way. The deputy followed. Ware led the way to that bench upon which he had sat with the Mexican. He sat down, and slowly the deputy took position beside him. He seemed to be waiting for some sort of resentful demonstration from Ware.

"Heard what you said," commenced Ware abruptly. "If you feel that way, why it's all right with me. Rangers are too busy working to have time for gabbing." His lifted hand checked the deputy, who had leaned slightly forward with lean, deep-lined face reddening. "Wait a minute! I'm a Texas Ranger . . . you're a deputy sheriff. Just admitted you aren't scared of anything. Bragged you'd go anywhere a ranger'd go. All right. If you wanted a man . . . a Mexican who was in Concepción . . . would you . . . I wonder if you'd go get him?"

"Yuh're damn' right!" the deputy cried hotly.

A corner of Ware's thin mouth lifted skeptically.

"I shore would!" the deputy insisted. "Or two or three or four Mexicans!"

Ware stared hard at him, then. "Believe you would," he said. "But it's a two-man job for choice . . . isn't it?"

The deputy nodded, but he wore a puzzled frown. "Whut's this all about?" he wanted to know.

"Ever have luck getting Mexican officials over there to give you a Mexican wanted over here?"

"Any time *they* turn one over to us!" The deputy laughed scornfully.

"What I thought," nodded Ware absently. "What I thought. And there's one in Concepción right now I sure want. Worth eight hundred . . . up at Vaca."

"Eight hund'd!" The deputy looked interested. "How come?"

"Assault to murder. Name's Gomez. Horseface Gomez. Happened this-a-way. Old Man Grimes . . . who used to own the Ladder D . . . he moved into town. Sold the ranch, lock, stock, and barrel, two, three weeks ago. Horseface heard Grimes'd have ten thousand dollars in his house that night. Busted in, tied up Grimes and old Miz Grimes. Like to beat the old man to death trying to make him tell where the money was. But the old man's a hardcase. Besides, that was all the money he had in the world. Horseface got scared off . . . people coming. Skipped out to the stable, cinched the old man's saddle onto the best horse there, and wandered into Mexico. Well, I found out, today, that Horseface is clerking in his cousin's store in Concepción. You got nerve enough to go where *this* ranger's going?"

Without hesitation the deputy nodded. "We split the eight hund'd?" he inquired cautiously.

"Sure do!" agreed Ware.

"Then when do we start?" the deputy asked briefly.

"Tonight. Mexican I know is living over there now. Got a cabin in the *bosque,* couple miles other side of the river. We'll lay up there, at Manuel's, till noon. Most of the town'll be taking a *siesta* then."

The deputy nodded. "Good enough," he said. "My name's Gordon."

"Mine's Ware."

The sudden narrowing of Gordon's eyes told Ware that the deputy had heard his name, had heard either of the night when he had served as marshal of Las Tunas or of some other case in which he had figured.

After dark they crossed the wide, shallow river at a place Gordon knew, well above the regular ford, where a man must keep his horse turning and twisting to escape the quicksands that were masked by knee-deep yellow water. The horses scrambled up the sandy bank on the Mexican side and shook themselves like dogs.

"Well?" inquired Gordon. "Can yuh find this Manuel's cabin?"

"Reckon," said Ware. "Manuel says it sets back a piece from the regular trail to town. Let's go up the riverbank."

So they headed vaguely north in the moonless darkness, following the curving of the river through the brakes of tornillo and willow and cottonwood saplings until they came to the well-beaten trail leading to Concepción from the ford. They met nobody between the river and the mouth of a narrow trail that was marked by a large, white stone.

"This is it," said Ware. "Reckon Manuel put the rock there today."

Manuel came to the door of his pole-walled hut in response to Ware's low yell.

"Is anyone here?" demanded Ware in Spanish.

"No one, *señor*, save my woman and the *muchacho*," Manuel assured him. "Will you enter my poor house or do you tonight go . . . ?"

He broke off, with a suspicious glance at Gordon.

"No, it would be impossible to discover him tonight without giving the alarm. So, Manuel, with your permission, we will remain here, putting the horses back in the *bosque* until tomorrow midday. Then will we ride boldly into Concepción and. . . ."

He snapped his fingers, and Manuel clicked tongue against teeth with a sound that conveyed complete understanding.

Manuel's woman was a slender girl of sixteen or so. The *muchacho* Manuelito, was nearly eight, a bright-faced youngster who was, Manuel proclaimed proudly, an *Americano*, having been born on the other side of the river to his first wife. The boy was hugely interested in the Americans. Manuel talked to him as to another man. Ware was at first somewhat

144

annoyed when the youngster discussed with him gravely the taking of Horseface Gomez, but Manuel assured the ranger proudly that little Manuel was tight-mouthed—"like the mule at sight of a bridle bit," as he expressed it.

"*Sí, señor,*" Manuelito nodded grave endorsement of this. "I do not discuss the private affairs of my friends with any man."

They slept that night back in the *bosque,* Manuelito in his blanket nearby. When dawn came, the boy brought them breakfast from the cabin, and they stayed in the brush during the warm forenoon for fear that some townsman might visit Manuel.

Gordon spoke seldom, and Ware was taciturn by nature. Manuelito talked gravely of men and things as he had seen them in Concepción or had heard them discussed by his father—who was this morning loafing about Concepción to make sure that Ware would find Horseface in the Gomez store at noon.

Eleven o'clock came. Gordon was beginning to fidget, but Ware squatted on his heels in the tiny shade of a cottonwood sapling, his bearing as patient as an Indian's.

"My father comes," Manuelito announced suddenly, and Ware turned a slow head, his hand slipping beneath the edge of his jumper to cuddle the stock of a Colt. Manuel came pushing through the brush.

" '*Sta bueno,*" he grinned nervously. "He will be there when you reach the *tienda. ¡Válgame Dios!* I am not precisely a coward, *señor,* but there is in the eyes of Horseface that which makes me to shiver! *Sí.* He would cut the throat of a man with no more thought than I would have for the crushing of an ant."

"He is a very bad man," nodded Manuelito gravely. "But we must not be afraid of him, my father."

Manuel had brought them food—warm tortillas spread with white cheese, a small, tin bucket of fat brown beans, and the inevitable inky coffee. They ate in silence, then Ware rose, and wiped his hands upon his trousers.

"Ready?" he asked. Gordon nodded silently.

As they swung into the saddles, Manuel and his son followed to Ware's stirrup.

"You will not forget?" Ware asked, staring hard into the Mexican's face.

Manuel lifted a shoulder and grinned, half ruefully: "No, *señor*," he promised. "Whatever comes of it, I will not forget."

"We will not forget," Manuelito echoed.

They rode by a trail Manuel had pointed out, a dim, narrow path made by the grubbers for mesquite roots that wound through the *bosque* paralleling the broader track from ford to village. So near noon they came abreast of Concepción, but hidden from it by the brush. They circled the straggling collection of adobes and so came jogging calmly into the place from its west side—just as if arriving from the interior of Mexico. It was the *siesta* hour, and the single crooked track that was Concepción's chief thoroughfare was almost deserted. A few horses dozed before house doors; mangy curs drowsed in shady spots; in the center of the street an enormous sow snored with her litter of piglets about her.

Ware knew from Manuel's description which was the store of Antonio Gomez, cousin of Horseface, the killer. Gordon, too, knew the place, for he had been in Concepción before. It was merely a flat-fronted adobe building, rather larger than those about it and with a door set across the blunted corner of the two street walls.

They drew rein before the door. Ware shifted slightly in

146

the saddle and regarded the deputy thoughtfully. Gordon's lean, deep-lined face was calm and inward.

Ware gave tribute to the deputy. Evidently he was no empty boaster. "Watch the horses, will you?" he queried. "I'll go in. Maybe I'll yell for you from the back . . . *quién sabe?* Be a-listening."

Gordon nodded, and, when Ware swung down, he followed suit and looked to the girths on both saddles. Ware nodded approval and went clicking inside the store. It was a single, long room, dusky, for the only windows were two small loopholes high up, one in each side wall. A rude counter ran the length of it. Upon its top were piles of vivid blankets, cheap cotton clothing, baskets of onions, and other groceries. From the cottonwood rafters hung strings of red chili and slabs of dried meat. Well down the counter a stocky Mexican of long, sullen face was measuring calico for a fat, barefooted old woman. In the rear of the store squatted, or sat with backs to the wall, three men who were drowsing.

Horseface Gomez lifted his head at the sound of Ware's boot heels, and the ranger, meeting that fixed, snaky regard, understood Manuel's instinctive fear of the man. He himself would have marked the Mexican instantly as one to watch, even without knowledge of the several killings charged to Horseface's account in Texas. The outlaw's two hands, holding the calico, were motionless. As Ware came down the long room, Horseface merely kept his black eyes steadily, with what seemed to be an habitual, unconscious watchfulness, upon the stranger. Neither the old woman nor any of the drowsing trio had seemed to notice Ware's entrance. Coming up beside the woman, Ware looked across the counter at Horseface.

"I am told," said Ware in accentless Spanish, face expressionless, "that you have a fine horse and saddle."

Horseface stared at him for an instant in silence, his eyes narrowed slightly. Ware knew that his instinctive suspicion of a stranger was now battling in the outlaw's mind with puzzlement concerning his, Ware's, nationality.

"They are not for sale," said Horseface curtly.

"Even so, may I see them, no?"

"No!" said Horseface curtly.

One hand—the right—began to slide forward toward the edge of the counter. But Ware's hand, too, moved flashingly. Horseface stared furiously down at the long-barreled Colt that menaced him across the counter. The old woman, who had gaped uncomprehendingly, now squealed shrilly and fell flat onto the floor in a faint. The three dozing men leaped to their feet to stare open-mouthed.

"Come with me," snapped Ware.

"Where?" countered Horseface. The fingers of his hand were working convulsively.

"Back to Texas. But, if that hand moves again, you will not go. You will stay in Concepción . . . forever. Raise your hands. Take hold of your ears. Quick, else I shoot. Now lead me to your horse."

For perhaps two seconds Horseface hesitated, his eyes flashing desperately about him, then Ware's thin lips parted slightly to show set teeth, and the big hammer beneath his thumb came back to full cock with a sinister click. Horseface gave in. Obediently he raised his hands to his ears and came around the counter end. Ware, with one eye upon the half-dazed, gaping Mexicans against the rear wall, ran an expert hand over the outlaw's person. He found a Colt beneath the shirt in the waistband of the trousers, a long-bladed knife in the sheath that hung down between his shoulder blades.

"Hurry, now," he commanded, and prodded his prisoner with Colt muzzle.

148

Horseface led him through a rear door. Across the yard was a rude stable. In this stable yard the outlaw turned to the right and would have marched toward another house forty yards away.

"Stop," demanded Ware. "What is in this stable here?"

"Nothing," grunted Horseface. "My horse is tied behind the house yonder."

"Ah," smiled Ware tightly. "But what if someone has played the joke upon you . . . has put your horse in the stable? Let us see and, remember, Horseface, if you die here for making a sudden sound, or giving me undue trouble, you cannot go with me back to Texas."

Sullenly Horseface moved toward the stable and without further protest preceded Ware inside. There stood a splendid, long-legged bay and upon a peg hung a silver-mounted saddle.

"Quickly now!" snapped Ware. "Saddle as if your life depended upon swiftness . . . for, indeed, it does!"

From behind him in the store Ware could hear excited chattering. Then, from a distance, came a shrill yell. One of those men who had been in the *tienda* was doubtless giving the alarm, he thought. Horseface heard, too. His efforts to bridle the bay were very fumbling. He leaped into the air with a startled oath as a bullet struck the ground at his feet, throwing dust over his rawhide sandals.

"The next one will kill," Ware assured him earnestly.

Horseface saddled hastily. Ware backed to the door with gun at hip level, covering Horseface. He raised his voice in a shrill yell, and instantly the rattle of shots sounded from the front of the store. Then, with a pounding of hoofs, Gordon, the deputy, came around the building and slid the horses to a halt.

"They're gangin' up in the street by the church," he said

calmly, working the ejector on his Colt. "Git him?"

Ware nodded. "Come out, Horseface. Bring the horse out," he ordered.

Gordon reloaded his Colt. Ware swung into the saddle, and at his command Horseface did the same.

"Cover him," snapped Ware to Gordon.

He jammed his gun back into the holster and drew his hunting knife, pushed Rocket over against Horseface's bay, and sheared away two rawhide tie-ties from the saddle. Roughly he seized Horseface's wrists and bound them together with the thongs.

"All right!" he snapped.

Before they had more than rammed home the spurs, the old bell of Concepción church began to clang. As they spurred out of the little stable yard—Ware in the lead, gripping the reins of the bay, and Gordon bringing up the rear—a horde of Mexicans came swarming around the store. They were armed with a motley array of ancient smooth-bores, old rifles, decrepit pistols. They fired frantically upon the Americans and the prisoner. Gordon turned in the saddle, sending a hail of bullets into the ground before them, and they gave back.

Still the church bell clanged, clanged, clanged.

Ware whirled around a house, into the trail to the ford. He turned in his saddle and saw the Mexicans downstreet flinging themselves upon their horses. The trail led through sand up to the animals' fetlocks, making the going slow, spur as they might. They had so little start that the bullets of the Mexicans, who were firing as fast as they could reload in the saddle, whined around their ears or kicked up the sand too close about them for comfort—and it was five long miles to the river. Still they managed to maintain their lead of a hundred yards or so—until Horseface hurled himself sideways from the saddle. Ware whirled Rocket instantly with a swirl of sand.

"Keep 'em back," he snapped to Gordon, and the deputy, jerking his lean gray about while he whipped a carbine from its saddle scabbard, opened fire upon the Mexicans.

While they stopped, milling excitedly, Ware rode up over Horseface, who was rolling sideways toward the brush. Ware lifted his Colt a trifle and with the report Horseface grunted painfully. There was a jagged hole through his right ear.

"Up! Back to your horse!" snarled Ware, motioning with the Colt.

Horseface scrambled to his feet and with face a furious mask threw himself into the saddle again.

"All right," said Ware calmly to Gordon.

Once more they took up the race. But now Horseface's bay began to limp. They were almost abreast of Manuel's cabin in the *bosque*. Whether or not the outlaw was responsible for this sudden lameness there was no way of telling, and Ware wasted no time on speculation. He yelled to Gordon, and, with the deputy quirting the bay and Ware hauling it forward, they managed to make the path toward Manuel's. The Mexicans were no more than fifty yards behind when the trio whirled down the narrow trail.

"Come on! Quirt the bay some more!" yelled Ware to Gordon.

The deputy pounded the limping animal's rump until he broke at last into a lumbering gallop. Up to Manuel's cabin they came, concealed for a moment from their pursuers by a bend in the trail. Around in the rear Ware led the way, fell back beside Horseface, eyed the outlaw calculatingly, then shot home his hard fist in a terrific hook that landed beneath the bleeding ear.

Horseface reeled sideways from the saddle, then Ware set

spurs to Rocket and, regardless of Gordon's bellows behind him, tugged the bay onward, cutting helter-skelter through the brush.

Now the Mexicans had caught sight of them again. Bullets buzzed spitefully about them, snapping leaves from cottonwood and willow. But twisting and turning through the dense growth, they saw the fugitives only for an instant.

The river was now in sight. Ware reached the ford by which they had come the night before and splashed down into the water. Gordon followed. They were in midstream when the pursuers reached the bank. The Mexicans, with howls of rage, fairly rained bullets after them, but the distance was too great for such weapons as theirs.

Rocket scrambled out on the Texas side, hauling the bay up after him. Ware turned in the saddle and doffed his sombrero in ironical salute and farewell to the Mexicans, Gordon, thin face bitterly contemptuous, spurred up beside him.

"You're a fine 'un!" he snapped furiously. "Let a passel o' Mexicans skeer yuh into lettin' go yo' man. By God! If I'd had a fifteen-year-old kid along with me, I'd've stopped an' chased them 'ere Mexicans clean back to Mexico City. An' yuh're one o' them rangers we hear tell so much about. Just like I said . . . a bunch o' four-flushers. Yuh make me sick!"

Ware eyed him thoughtfully, without resentment. "I *sabe* how you feel. But one thing a ranger knows," he drawled, "is it's better to get away yourself than to sure get killed trying to hang onto an eight-hundred-dollar Mexican. They were too close and getting closer. If Horseface's bay hadn't gone lame, might've taken a chance."

"Aw, hell!" spat Gordon. "S'pose yuh brought along the hoss to show on this side so's yuh can brag yuh got his hoss, anyhow."

Ware shrugged and turned up the riverbank. There was a big bend in the river here, densely wooded on either side. For a mile or more Ware led the way along the shore, then suddenly he pulled Rocket to a halt and stared across toward the Mexican shore. Gordon, mechanically looking also, stiffened in his saddle.

For, wading across the stream toward them, came Horseface Gomez, still with his hands bound before him. In his wake strutted Manuelito, prodding the meek outlaw with a thorny branch. Manuel on a burro brought up the rear, an old rifle across his arm.

Ware looked out of the corner of his eye at Gordon. "I figured maybe we couldn't get out of Concepción without the Mexicans being right on our tail," he drawled. "Of course, I never looked for the bay to go lame, but in the rangers, Gordon, you have to learn to figure on everything. So I fixed it up with Manuel there. If we were too hard pressed, we'd try to make his cabin and hand over Horseface for him to sneak over if he could, while we'd get away without the Mexicans knowing we didn't still have Horseface. Never said anything to you about it, because there was a chance Manuel couldn't get him out of sight of the Mexicans that were following us. Now, you're a deputy sheriff for this county. Yonder comes Horseface Gomez. He's wanted up at Vaca. If I were you, I'd sure arrest him and collect that eight hundred dollars reward. Then I'd split it with Manuel."

Gordon stared blankly. "But you . . . ," he began.

"Never mind!" cried Ware impatiently. "Better this way . . . arrest being made on the American side. Me, I'll take back Old Man Grimes's horse and his saddle. He's a mighty fine old fella, Grimes. He did me a favor once I won't ever forget."

Horseface came stumbling up the bank and sank down in a wet and weary heap before them. Manuelito followed him and nodded to the silent Americans.

"Here is the man, *señores*," he reported gravely.

"But . . . ," Gordon began with a puzzled frown.

"Never mind now," said Ware.

A tiny smile showed at his lip corner as from its sheath he drew his knife. While all three watched him curiously, he crossed to the bay, caught up a corner of the saddle skirt, and split the thread that held the sheepskin pad to the skirt proper. Under his fingers the two thicknesses of the skirt yawned like the end of an open envelope. Slowly Ware probed in the opening and brought out a sweat-stained banknote. Another and another.

"All together," he said thoughtfully, "there's ten thousand dollars in that saddle. Horseface did his damnedest to get that money from Grimes and . . . he did it, too, you see!" He grinned at the gaping Horseface. "So, Gordon, you-all take Horseface and split that eight hundred with Manuel. I'll take back the money to Old Man Grimes. Like I said, he did me a favor once, and, when I heard about this business, I promised him I'd sure get his money back for him if I had to chase this saddle clean to Mexico City."

"How much reward's he goin' to give yuh?" asked Gordon.

"I said," Ware's tone was suddenly frosty, "that Old Man Grimes is a *friend* of mine."

" 'Scuse me!" cried Gordon. "My mistake! An' . . . an' . . . forgit what I was sayin' about the rangers, will yuh? I feel sort o' different right now, havin' rid into some powder smoke with one of the outfit."

Blotting the Triangle

The white road was as curved as a dozing snake. In places it was a hundred yards wide; again it narrowed to a tenth of that width and was hard-beaten by the hoofs of many horses and cattle. Rocket, Ware's tall black stallion, sometimes kicked up a cloud of chalky dust, then coughed as it tickled his throat. At which Ware grinned faintly, for the sound reminded him of Miss Lee, the old maid who kept a boarding house near the plaza in El Paso. It was Miss Lee's habit to cough disapprovingly at such actions of her boarders as her New England training could not condone.

"Quit your coughing," he counseled Rocket. "Your mind's getting off our business, fella. Way you act, we got till kingdom come to get to Smithville."

Rocket cocked one sensitive ear toward his small rider and shifted from running-walk to fox-trot. Presently he came to where, at a clump of mesquite, a narrow trail came into the road, and from behind the mesquite came a horse, a white-faced bay, as tall as Rocket, carrying a big, dark, hook-nosed man.

Ware reined in, as did the other. For an instant they sat looking each other over with the guarded and expressionless curiosity proper to the time and place. Ware had the advantage at this trick that his steady, gray-green eyes and his lean, brown face rarely showed any more emotion than would have a Comanche. There were rangers who had known him rather intimately during his three years in the service who had never

157

seen him smile. So he sat Rocket in negligent posture, a smallish figure in wide-brimmed and bullion-trimmed Mexican sombrero, short jacket of soft-tanned goatskin fringed to the elbow, and bell-bottomed trousers of fine blue wool with rows of silver buttons bordering the scarlet insert of the outer seams. He wore no visible weapons, but a sleek Winchester carbine was in the saddle scabbard.

The hook-nosed man grinned finally. He was rather handsome, with strong white teeth showing. Something of a dandy in his dress—forty-dollar Stetson, white silk shirt, skin-tight trousers of fawn-colored cloth tucked carefully into the polished tops of expensive boots. His saddle, too, was a costly hull, hand-stamped and silver-mounted. He wore a silver-plated Colt on right thigh.

"Howdy, Ranger," he said cordially. "Headin' for town?"

Ware nodded silently and tickled Rocket with a spur rowel. The big man turned the bay in beside the black stallion and shifted his weight to his left stirrup, to face Ware, the better to talk.

"How's business?" he grinned. "You're the fella they call Ware, ain't you? Thought so. That outfit o' yours . . . an' your horse, too . . . make you easy to recognize. Well, I reckon there ain't much to worry about, up in this part o' the country. Smithville's right peaceful, mostly. Wasn't always that way, they tell me. I'm from up Red River way. Got the JM outfit east o' here now. Bought her three year back. But, like I was sayin', when old Hen Smith first built a tradin' store here, she was pretty well uncurried."

He chuckled to himself, seeming unconcerned by his companion's silence.

"He was a right organized old hairpin, Hen Smith, from what I hear. Come a time when the settlement was feelin' her oats a bit. Some of the folks figured she ought to have a better name than Smithville. Said that was too damn o'n'ry.

" 'O'n'ry!' howls Hen Smith, yankin' his Bowie knife an' flippin' her into a dry-goods box. 'How come she's o'n'ry? Ain't no place in Texas got a more different name. She's spelled S-m-x-t-h-v-i-l-l-e, an,' if any gent here 'lows *that's* o'n'ry, I do hope as how he'll step up right now an' le' me talk it over with him!' "

"Restaurant?" inquired Ware.

They were in sight of the two straggling rows of buildings that fenced the two sides of the road and made Smithville of the usual spelling.

"Two of 'em," nodded the hook-nosed man. "Chinese joint right ahead. Cooks wonderful meals, but he don't cook 'em right. Better tie into the UanMe. That's Harry Bowers's grub emporium. They got a black cook that *is* a cook an' "— he winked expressively at Ware—"there's somethin' there that's worth lookin' at. Still . . . Miz Bowers kind o' leans toward dudes. Right now, it's Art Haskell. He's cashier o' the Stockmen's Bank, an' he wears a hard hat. Don't know . . . maybe you could beat his time."

Ware stared thoughtfully ahead. There were adobes set off the road here and there, the houses of townsmen, Mexican and white. On the road's edge, the first building on the left was the restaurant of the Chinaman, Sing Lee. Beyond the Chinaman's the **White Elephant** saloon, gambling house, and dance hall stretched its extensive front. Then there was the **Square Deal** store and next to it the **UanMe**. Directly across the road from the Bowers' restaurant was the **Stockmen's Bank**, a squat brown adobe.

As the pair jogged into town, a slender woman stood beneath a cottonwood before the UanMe, with beside her one who could be none other than the bank cashier, Art Haskell, for derby hats were few and far between in the cow-country in that day.

"Told you!" grinned Ware's companion. "Art Haskell's either got lots o' sand or damn' few brains. If I was chasin' a man's wife, I sure wouldn't ever stand out on the street in daylight, honeyin' up to her. Not with her man a-cloudin' up day by day like Harry Bowers is doin'. No, sir!"

He shifted a trifle more in the saddle so that he stared straight at Ware. His face had suddenly turned serious.

"Tell you what, Ware. I said a while back that Smithville's right peaceful. Well, I wasn't thinkin' about this here three-cornered deal when I said it. I'm tellin' you straight . . . there's goin' to be powder burnt in this street here an' 'tain't goin' to be long, neither. Haskell an' Nellie Bowers is gettin' opener an' opener, an' Harry Bowers is about due to cut loose. Watch an' see."

"Nothing to me," shrugged Ware indifferently. "Troubles of my own. Going to eat. Come along?"

"Reckon not. Later, maybe. Stayin' in town tonight?"

"Don't know. Maybe."

"Well, come on down to the White Elephant when you've et. I'll be there. Oh! I'm Jake Mitchell. That's where the JM comes from in my brand. Well, see you some more!"

Haskell, the bank cashier, looked up quickly as Ware reined in Rocket almost at his elbow. He was a heavy-set man in the late twenties with smooth, pale face and weak blue eyes. There was about him a certain chilly air of importance, as if he felt that his official position in the bank required him to hold somewhat aloof from the general run of the world's people.

Ware rather disliked him at first glance. Not only because of what Jake Mitchell had said of his relations with the restaurant owner's wife, but because of his personal appearance.

But he gave no sign of this, merely swung down and doffed his sombrero to the woman.

She was watching him rather curiously—a shapely blonde woman of twenty-four or -five, with an expression of weariness marring the prettiness of her regular features and large blue eyes.

"Eat?" inquired Ware respectfully. "Horse, too."

She nodded silently and turned toward the restaurant door with Ware studying her unobtrusively. At her call, a Mexican boy appeared.

"I'll feed him," said Ware. "Show me where."

He came back from the corral at the rear of the restaurant to find Haskell gone. Mrs. Bowers was behind the rough, unpainted counter with round, bare arms resting upon it. Her steady gaze at him made Ware vaguely uncomfortable.

He ordered his meal—it was nearing sundown now—and she repeated the list in a singsong chant to the cook without moving from her position within arm's length of him. Deliberately he made a cigarette and lit it.

"You came in with Jake Mitchell," she said suddenly.

He nodded.

"Do you know him?" she asked with eyes steadily on his brown face.

"Met him uptrail. Told me his name. Told me lots of things. About the town."

"Jake's quite a conversationalist," she remarked slowly. "But there isn't anything to tell about Smithville. It's just a dull little place where nothing happens. Back East, where we're from, it's different. . . ."

She stared past him now, with widened eyes, as if she looked through the wall at those distant places. Came the *whang* of a rifle outside, followed instantly by the vicious roar

161

of a Colt. Ware's left arm jerked; he pushed the woman below the counter top and himself skated across to peer cautiously through a window. A white-handled Colt had appeared, as by legerdemain, from beneath his jumper. He lifted it to the window sill.

A man stood almost against the restaurant wall outside with a long-barreled revolver in his hand. A wisp of smoke curled slowly from its muzzle. Across the street, a man lay face downward in the white dust, with a Winchester a yard beyond him. He was quite still. Men appeared and gathered about the fallen one; the victor of the duel watched them for an instant, then went cautiously across to join them. Ware came back to the counter. The woman now stood in the door. She, too, returned to her position.

"Ike Jenkins has been hunting Tom Warner for two weeks," she said tonelessly. "Well, he found him. Tom's rather deadly with a Colt."

Then she noted the thin trickle of blood running down Ware's sleeve.

"That bullet struck you!" she said. "I thought it had merely gone between us. I'll fix it for you."

"Never mind," said Ware hastily. "Just a burn. It's all right."

But she paid no attention to his protests. She disappeared into the kitchen and came back after a moment with a tin washpan filled with hot water.

"Take off that jumper," she commanded. Then, with a slow smile: "My Lord, boy. I'm not going to hurt you."

Obediently Ware slipped out of the fringed jumper. Her eyes narrowed a trifle at sight of the twin white-handled Colts slung deftly for a cross-arm draw in the John Wesley Hardin holsters. But she said nothing, merely rolled up the flannel shirt sleeve and washed the place where the heavy .45-70 had grazed the arm. Then she bandaged it quite expertly.

"Thanks," mumbled Ware. He finished his meal as rapidly as possible, paid his dollar, and went out.

In front of the Square Deal store, he stopped irresolutely. He had intended to ride on after the meal, to sleep wherever he decided to stop along the trail. But now—he wondered why he should be of two minds about going on. There was nothing he could do in this business. He might feel vaguely grateful to the woman for her small kindliness to him, but how could he interfere in this triangular mess? If she chose to carry on with the cashier, Haskell, at risk of rousing her husband to a shooting, there seemed little or nothing an outsider could do. She had impressed Ware as knowing quite well what she wanted.

She'll get what she's after . . . whatever it is, he thought. Then he shrugged impatiently and went on the few steps to the White Elephant. It was a large place, a square room divided by a partition paralleling the street. The long front room was so made that the partition separated the saloon proper from the gambling room. The other half of the building was the dance hall. It being the evening meal hour, there were few at the bar in the saloon, but voices sounded in the gambling room. Ware strolled over to the door and looked in. Jake Mitchell and two middle-aged cowmen were playing poker. Ware moved to a position where he could watch. He had never touched a card in his life, but he owned the common human fascination in games of chance.

He had been watching but a moment or two, unnoticed, when Jake Mitchell won a small pot and stretched luxuriously. "Goin' to grab me some supper whilst I'm winner enough to pay for her," he grinned, getting up. "Be back after while an' give you-all a chance to win back what the Chinaman leaves."

He saw Ware and nodded.

"Been havin' a streak o' luck, Ranger. These here gamboliers . . . they're worse'n the Sam Bass outfit. They don't need no guns to get the money."

He went out, a fine figure of a cowman. The eyes of the older men with whom he had played followed him half-humorously, half-pityingly.

"Jake's a right good boy," drawled one. "But in lots o' ways he's shore hare-brained. Easy-goin' an' all, good cowman, but . . . well, he ain't the first 'n' ever gambled away an outfit."

"Heerd he's a half-breed," remarked the other player. "An yuh know how Injuns is . . . bet high, wide, an' handsome on which way a flea'll jump. Reckon that streak o' red in Jake gives him his gamblin' craze."

They sat comfortably, gossiping of this small thing and that. Ware squatted on his heels in an out-of-the-way corner. He was more than ever of two minds as to going on. He scowled at his boot toes and smoked. *Isn't a damn' thing to keep me,* he thought. *No use being sentimental about the Bowers woman. Ought to get Rocket and get out.*

Still, he was there when Jake Mitchell came back from Sing Lee's and, with a humorous wolf howl, announced himself heaven-elected to take the scalps of all Smithville gamblers into camp with him. The two cowmen declined further poker, but others—habitués of the White Elephant, Ware thought—sat down with the big JM owner. A half hour passed, with Ware quiet in his corner and Jake Mitchell's pile of chips melting steadily.

The two grizzled cowmen with whom Jake Mitchell had played before supper sat near enough to Ware for him to overhear their low-toned conversation. They were watching Jake Mitchell's flushed face, his hands that fed the house men of the White Elephant regularly from his chips.

"Made a raise when he went to supper," guessed one—he who had remarked upon Mitchell's mixed blood. "Reckon that three, fo' hund'd just about cleans out the li'l ol' JM. Heerd that Jim Thompson's shut down on Jake. Bank's about owned the outfit for a couple months."

"Thompson's a good man as well as a good banker," shrugged his companion. "Reckon he must've staked Jake tonight out o' his own pocket. 'Cause when he clamps down official, as pres'dent o' the Stockmen's Bank, he's shore clamped."

Jake Mitchell rose with a short, mirthless laugh. He held out his hands, empty palms significantly upturned. "That'll be all for this performance," he told the house men ruefully. "Well, gents, see you-all some more. Got a powwow to make with my banker."

Ware nodded in return to Jake Mitchell's good night. The two old cowmen were still sitting nearby. He got up and moved unobtrusively over beside them, and murmured a greeting.

"These Bowers folks," he drawled, "they of the Santone Bowerses? Ate there tonight, but didn't see Bowers."

"Don' know if they be Santone folks," the elder man replied thoughtfully. "Harry Bowers has got weak lungs, an' he's livin' down here 'cause o' that. They keep to the'selves right smart. Harry'll be in fo' his nightcap right away. Comes in ever' night about this time."

"Thanks," nodded Ware.

He wandered restlessly about, pausing finally at the rear door of the big dance hall. Standing so, staring outside into the pale moonlight, he could see the corral at the rear of the UanMe restaurant. As he watched aimlessly, he noted a woman hurrying from the Bowers' house, which was at the

165

restaurant's rear, to the corral beyond. For a moment, he thought it was Mrs. Bowers, but closer scrutiny betrayed the shuffling gait of a Mexican woman. She carried a bundle and disappeared into the corral with it. Ware watched, wondering. Then she reappeared, leading a horse. The bundle was now behind the saddle. She tied the horse to a corral rail, looked around quickly, then hastened back toward the Bowers' house. Ware's eyes narrowed. He scraped a boot toe nervously across the floor. Then, making up his mind, he slid from the doorway and went soundlessly toward the corral, keeping in the shadow of the rear wall of the Square Deal store.

He crossed swiftly to the corral and touched the bundle. It was soft. He probed into it through a gap in the folded sheet that wrapped it. The ruffled hem of a skirt came into view. He searched further and found more clothing, woman's clothing, and little trinkets. Satisfied as to the bundle's contents, he straightened it and moved swiftly and silently toward the Bowers' house.

He hardly knew what he intended to do, what he planned to say to Mrs. Bowers. There was a lighted window in the house front wall, and he went noiselessly up to where he could peer in. There was the Mexican woman, making a corn shuck cigarette, but no sign of Mrs. Bowers. Ware went back to the door and knocked gently.

"*¿Quién es?*" inquired the Mexican woman after a lengthy moment. "Who is it?"

"A friend!" replied Ware in Spanish. "One wishing speech with you, *señora*."

The door opened a crack, and Ware promptly thrust his boot toe into it but smiled reassuringly at the woman.

"Your mistress? I wish to talk to her."

"She is at the restaurant, *señor*. At this hour her husband goes usually to the saloon and leaves her in charge of the place."

Ware hesitated a moment, then pushed the door open, slipped inside, and closed it after him. The woman shrank away, eyes widened fearfully.

"Why did you place *la señora*'s clothing behind the saddle of that horse?" demanded Ware, now grim of face. "Answer! I'm a ranger, and it is in my hands to take you to prison for theft."

"I . . . my mistress ordered it," stammered the woman. "I am but her servant. It is not for me to ask the reason for her orders."

Ware studied her silently, gray-green eyes narrowed, brown face ugly of expression—for it was an unpleasant situation into which he had thrust himself, and he was by no means pleased now with his own forwardness.

Suddenly the woman threw up both hands with palms placatingly outward: "I will tell the truth, *señor!*" she cried. "Only do not take me to prison. I have tiny children. It would kill me to leave them."

"Quick, then," he snapped, seizing the advantage.

"It was the *señor* who once troubled my mistress with his attentions . . . *Señor* Mitchell. He told me that he but played a joke upon her and paid me three dollars to saddle my mistress's horse and place the bundle of clothing behind the saddle. He . . . *¡Madre de Dios!* . . . what was that?"

It was a single pistol shot in the street. Ware waited tensely for another, but there was none. He whirled and jerked open the door and slid out. In such a frontier town as Smithville, a single shot was more expressive than might have been a fusillade—for the latter indicated, frequently, no more than the arrival of exuberant cowboys from some distant ranch, heralding their approach by the time-honored double roll. He ran down the rear walls of the buildings on that side of the street until he could dart between two stores and peer out. On the wide, adobe-pillared verandahs of the White Elephant saloon and the Square Deal store he made out dark masses of men. A single figure lay sprawled before the door of the UanMe restaurant. Otherwise the pale, moonlit street was empty.

He ran swiftly across the street and slipped between buildings there to their rear, then went very cautiously past the New York store, past the house of Jim Thompson, president of the Stockmen's Bank—noting that it was lighted—and so to the back of the house of Haskell, the bank cashier, and from Haskell's corral came the snorting of a horse.

Ware glanced that way and made out the dim shape of the animal. It was outside the corral, and he slipped over to it. Even in the dim moonlight he could see a bundle beside the cantle. As he touched it, he noted a sack lying limply across the saddle seat. He rammed his hand into its yielding surface; there was the crisp rustle of paper. A moment's exploration informed him that packages of banknotes were in the sack. Clothing was in the slicker-wrapped bundle behind the saddle.

He frowned, standing there in the shadow of the horse. Then he made a little clucking sound, indicative of decision, and darted across to Haskell's back door. It was fastened by a wooden latch, and softly he lifted the latch trigger. Inside, he saw through the crack, was a Mexican boy of sixteen or so.

The boy turned flashingly, his hand going toward his open shirt neck. But a Colt jumped into Ware's hand. Fearfully the boy waited, with no further hostile move.

"What were you paid to saddle that horse . . . to make that bundle of your master's clothing . . . and put it behind the saddle?"

168

"Two dollars, *señor*," answered the boy mechanically. He stared at Ware as if at something uncanny.

"Then *Señor* Mitchell owes you a dollar," said Ware solemnly. "For he paid the woman of the *Señora* Bowers three dollars to do the same thing. Why did he wish this done?"

"For a jest, he said," shrugged the boy. "If there was wrong in doing it, I am not to blame. He threatened to beat me if I did not help him play this trick upon *mi patrón*."

Ware nodded and was gone through the door like a shadow. Men were ahead of him now, running toward the yellow rectangle that was the open rear door of the bank. There was much loud talking. Ware could make nothing intelligible from what he heard. He followed them and stood in the doorway of the bank, looking in upon the scene of confusion.

Inside the wire-partitioned space given over to the bank's office a table was overturned. Bills and silver and a few pieces of gold were upon the floor. The door of the big iron safe was open. But what riveted Ware's attention was the group of men who held Haskell, the bank cashier—a pasty-faced, wild-eyed Haskell. He was shouting something. It sounded like a protestation of innocence, but the clamor of the men around him made it gibberish.

Now, from just inside the front door, a young cowboy raised a discovery whoop. He came pushing through the men about Haskell, holding up a short-barreled, heavy-calibered, single-action Colt. "The bank pistol!" he yelled. "One ca'tridge shot, too."

"His hoss was saddled an' tied to the corral!" shouted another man. "An' we found this sack lyin' acrost it. An' his clothes was in the slicker behind the saddle."

A big man, Renfrew of the Square Deal store, caught the arm of that young cowboy who had the bank pistol, pulled him to his side, and whispered in his ear. The cowboy listened, jerked his head sideways to stare up at the big storekeeper.

"By God!" he cried. "I wonder. . . ."

He whirled back toward the front door and elbowed his way through the press. Going out, he collided with Jake Mitchell and a leathery-faced man of sixty or so—Jim Thompson, the retired cowman who was president of the bank. The crowd drew back to let the pair come through. They watched the banker curiously, seeming to wait, to look to him for action. Ware came on inside. The luminous, almost electric glow that was, with him, signal of approaching action showed in the depths of gray-green eyes.

Jake Mitchell, at sight of the ranger, whispered to Jim Thompson. The old man stared curiously at the small figure in Mexican clothing, then held up his hand. "I don' know exactly what all the trouble's about," drawled Thompson. "I hear that Harry Bowers is shot . . . was shot from the bank door. But we got a ranger here, Jake Mitchell tells me. Seein's we got no marshal right now, I'd like to have the ranger sort o' take charge while we look things over."

Ware nodded briefly and came up to stand beside the banker.

Renfrew, the Square Deal owner, pushed up like a bull, glowering at the pallid Haskell. "Yore cashier shot Harry Bowers," he declared. "Five o' us was standin' on my verandah. We happened to all be lookin' this way. We seen Haskell in the door . . . yuh couldn't mistake him an' that fool hat of his across Texas . . . an' all of a sudden he lets go one. We looked to see what he was a-shootin at, an' Harry Bowers was keelin' over. Sam Bridges found the bank six-shooter on the floor by the front door, with the ca'tridge shot. Some o' the boys found Haskell's hoss tied to the corral with his clothes behind the saddle an' a sack o' money across the seat. An'. . . ."

Sam Bridges, the young cowboy, burst into the door. "Yuh was dead right, Renfrew!" he yelled. "Miz Bowers's hoss is tied to her corral. Her clothes is behind the saddle. They was figgerin' to rattle their hocks together, a' right."

The crowd's ugly mood was intensified as the significance of this report sank in. Men muttered to one another, cast grimly menacing glances at the shaken cashier. He shrank back before them. Another moment and there would have been a lariat produced, and it could have been too late to check the rush that would have taken Haskell outside to the nearest cottonwood.

But Ware held up his hand. "Folks," he called. "I haven't heard this fella's tale yet. Let's see what he's got to say. Speak up, fella."

"I didn't shoot Bowers!" cried Haskell shrilly. "I didn't rob the bank. I was working in here tonight, as I often do. Inside the cage there, at the table. I didn't hear a thing. Just felt a pistol muzzle in my back. Somebody whispered for me to keep still, said he'd shoot if I made the slightest sound. The bank pistol was in the drawer of the table, but I couldn't reach for it. The robber slipped my own handkerchief out of my coat pocket and blindfolded me. He pulled me up, turned me around. . . ."

"All right in plain sight o' the door," purred Renfrew. "Well, he must have been a blame amateur, Haskell."

"No. I forgot that. He had blown out the lamp on the table. He pushed me over to the safe and made me fill a sack with money . . . bills mostly. I knew by the bundles that he was getting ten or fifteen thousand dollars. Then he walked me out to the front door, and we stood there a long time. It seemed ages. Suddenly he shoved me to one side, so hard that

I staggered and fell against the wall over there in the corner. I heard him shoot. I jerked off the handkerchief, and I guess I hardly knew what I was doing. The next thing I remember was the crowd of you running in and grabbing me."

"That's exactly the way it happened, I bet," nodded Sam Bridges energetically. "But yuh plumb forgot how Santy Claus come down the chimbley just then, Haskell. Yuh hadn't ought to forget that-a-way."

"Le's see that sack o' money yuh-all found on Haskell's saddle," demanded Jim Thompson abruptly.

He opened it and shook it out upon the floor, knelt, and counted the bills. He counted them twice, then stood up, shaking his head.

"Le's see what's gone out of the safe," he grunted.

He pawed over the safe shelves for a while, then came out, the lines in his brown face seeming deeper.

"Folks, Haskell told the truth when he said ten or fifteen thousand was took out o' the safe. But there ain't but twenty-two hundred in that bag. Now, where's the rest? What d'yuh figger, Ranger?"

Ware looked about the half circle of grim faces; the glow was in his eyes, and a small, mirthless smile twitched the corners of his thin mouth. "Folks," he drawled solemnly, "this is a right tangled mess. The robber Haskell told about . . . he's a mighty slick hairpin an' a dangerous one, I reckon. Putting the iron into him's likely to be real risky."

Renfrew laughed harshly, and some of the others joined in uncertainly, but most of the citizenry of Smithville stared curiously at Ware. He pushed through to the whitewashed wall and drew a .45 cartridge from a jumper pocket. With this for pencil, he drew a rude equilateral triangle upon the wall, then turned, and looked the crowd over. He had their attention now.

"Mitchell, you know this town's lay-out," he stated. "Come here and give me a hand."

Jake Mitchell, grinning, came over and waited expectantly.

"The original brand I figured on this deal . . . ," said Ware, like a schoolmaster with the .45 shell poised in the air, "was the Triangle. But I see now that I've got to blot her and. . . ." He drew another equilateral triangle upon the first, so that the two, joined, made a rough square, albeit one pushed slightly out of plumb. He turned back to the room. "You see," he drawled, "triangles haven't but three points, and this deal's got four." He grinned at Jake Mitchell. "Mitchell, you owe that Mexican boy of Haskell's another dollar. 'Twasn't fair to pay Miz Bowers's woman three dollars to saddle her horse and tie it to the corral and just pay Haskell's boy two dollars for tying his horse out."

"What're you talkin' about?" cried Mitchell.

"About the robbery," Ware explained obligingly. "About how you figured you could get enough money to square yourself and kill Harry Bowers and get Haskell hung and dirty that lady's name all at the same crack, by having their horses tied to the corrals . . . to be found with their clothes tied to the cantles and a sack with a little bit of the bank money across Haskell's saddle. After you'd robbed the bank. . . . Ah! . . . thought you would!"

Mitchell had gone for his gun with the speed of a striking cat. But if the big man's hand moved flashingly, Ware's Colt came out so rapidly that the motion seemed blurred. He struck twice with the long barrel—once at Mitchell's wrist, again at his face. The 'breed's gun dropped to the floor, and he staggered, with blood bursting from a cut across the forehead. He was handcuffed before he had recovered from the blow.

"They all leave a hole open," Ware moralized. "Catching 'em's just a business of watching and piecing together the odds and ends you find. Trusting two outsiders . . . the Mexican servants of these folks . . . to plant those horses was Mitchell's slip-up. But it was sure a slick scheme."

"But where's the rest o' the money?" demanded old Jim Thompson.

"Where's Jake Mitchell's horse?" countered Ware confidently.

"In my corral. Yuh mean . . . ?"

"It ought to be in the saddlebags. This 'breed figured he'd stick around just long enough to see the fella he hated get his and the woman who'd chased him branded, then he'd ride off whistling with the money."

"Doc says Harry Bowers ain't going to die!" announced a hard-faced citizen, arriving now at the front door. "An', listen, folks! Yuh all know Kiowa Smith fer a man o' his word. Well, I'm promisin' that the first li'l word I ever hear about that lady, Miz Bowers, flirtin' with anybody but her husband is shore goin' to be a invite to me to come smokin'! I watched her a-croonin' over him like as if he's a baby, an' nobody can make me believe nothin' but good about her."

Renfrew, the big storekeeper, pushed up to Ware now, smiling grimly. "Well, Ranger," he said. "I reckon we'll send this varmint down to the county seat to stand trial. But if Harry Bowers had died, we would shore have done more'n blotted that triangle o' yours . . . we would have just plumb knocked hell out of it."

Ware Calls It a Day

Ware looked over the loafers and customers in Mel Murfree's general store and post office. Those inhabitants of Yantsboro who came under his green-gray regard were hardly aware of it; his rangering had taught him a good deal about diverse things, and he had a flashing, yet accurate, picture of cowman and sheep man, farmer and townsman in his head with hardly the seeming of having looked at them at all. The general store housed, also, the post office, for Yantsboro was one of those towns commonly known in west Texas as "a wide place in the road." The lines of frame and adobe buildings, with behind them a scattering of Mexican *jacales,* constituted Yants County's seat of authority as well as its trading place.

Ware attracted some attention here. Shadowing his lean, brown face was the wide brim of a great, silver-embroidered Mexican sombrero. He wore a *charro* jumper of goatskin fringed to the elbow and made gay by a bouquet of scarlet roses embroidered onto the back. His trousers were of fine blue woolen cut with loose bottoms that dropped low over handmade 'puncher's boots and with a strip of crimson between the rows of silver buttons along the outer seam. He wore no visible belt gun. His twin, white-handled Colts were slung crosswise in the holsters beneath his jumper, but, as he came into Murfree's, he carried across his arm a sleek Winchester carbine, carried it absently, as if unconsciously through long habit of its possession.

As he went quietly back toward the mail window in the

store's rear, a lean, hawk-faced young man got up from where he sat on a pickle keg. Ware caught the movement from the tail of his eye and stopped—apparently to examine a Navajo saddle blanket that hung from the wall. He had never seen the fellow before, and yet there moved in him a vague emotion that warned him of . . . —danger? He could not tell. But he did sense that somehow this cowboy was connected with him, that time would make clear the degree and kind of their relation for good or bad. And so he photographed the fellow mentally, where he stood beside a fat and shabby man whose nose blossomed magnificently purple in a red-veined face.

At the window he waited for the angular wife of Mel Murfree to come hurrying back to him. She lifted a hand toward the rude pigeonholes on her right and looked at him inquiringly.

"Mail for Ware?" he asked politely.

She drew out an envelope from a pigeonhole and held it uncertainly, pursing her thin lips. Ware understood. From inside his jumper somewhere he produced another envelope and showed its face to her. She handed over the letter, and Ware, with a nod of thanks, moved back to the dusky rear of the store and squatted beside the wall. He rolled a brown cigarette, staring thoughtfully at the unopened envelope upon his knee—but observing that the hawk-faced cowboy had gone out. When he had flicked a matchhead upon thumbnail and lit his cigarette, he opened the envelope and read:

Dear Ware:

    Stay in Yantsboro for the present. Ride herd on that place. Hewell, the present sheriff, is said to be a weak sister. He asked the governor for a ranger to watch things for a while. Nothing specific, said general conditions worried him. So use your own

**judgment and communicate with me if you don't
think conditions justify remaining. I have plenty of
work for you.**

The letter was signed by Captain Knowles.

Ware sat thoughtfully, reflecting that there was an under-
current here of which he knew nothing. For he had considered Yants County quite peaceful. Even the long, wild border
of it, the river separating it from Mexican territory, was not
infested more than that of neighboring counties with crimi-
nals. None of these counties had requested rangers. What
was there here that local peace officers could not handle?

He got up with what seemed a single, tigerish movement;
one moment he was squatting, the next he was standing erect.
Hewell, the "weak sister" sheriff, should be able to explain
the reasons for his request to the governor. As he went out
and stood on the store's gallery looking for the sheriff's office,
Ware was recalling what he had heard of Hewell. He knew
from the gossip of rangers and peace officers—who rarely talk
anything but shop between themselves—that old Sheriff
Childers had been killed going on two years before by Wynn
Eggers, who had some reputation as a gunman and around
whom clung sundry suspicions of cattle stealing. Two days
after Childers's death, Wynn Eggers had suddenly appeared
in Yantsboro. Eggers had been sought without success during
the intervening period. Hewell was acting sheriff, having
been Childers's sole deputy. He had encountered Eggers and
had shot the gunman through the shoulder, capturing him.
And Eggers's trial—at which he admitted killing Childers,
but claimed mistaken identity and self-defense—had sent the
gunman to the penitentiary for life.

Ware saw a faded little sign well up the street, announcing
the sheriff's office. He went that way and found that the two-

storied adobe building was Yants County courthouse, jail, and sheriff's office in one. The door to the office was open and inside sat a slender boy of sixteen or seventeen, practicing the "road agent's spin" with an ancient cap-and-ball Colt. He looked up at Ware with calm, blue eyes.

"Howdy, Ranger!" he greeted him. "Lookin' fer the sher'ff? Thought yuh was. Hewell thought yuh would be. He's gone . . . won't be back fer a couple of weeks. Left a note fer yuh."

Ware eyed him steadily. There was a sardonic amusement about the boy's face and tone, as he spoke of Sheriff Hewell.

"He saw yuh ride in," grinned the boy. "He says to me . . . 'There comes my ranger. Stephen Ware, from the Mex outfit, straddlin' that Swayn stallion. I ain't got time to talk to him. Got to make Brackett an' catch the train. Give him this here note.' Then he scribbled her an' high-tailed it out back to grab his hoss. Yuh won't see Hewell fer a spell."

Ware took the piece of wrapping paper and looked curiously at the scrawled single sentence that was Sheriff Hewell's departing message:

Got a kid sick in the hospital and got to go see him and you hold down things in Yantsboro till I get back couple weeks maybe more.

"Yuh're sher'ff, mister," grinned the kid. "I reckon ol' Bill Withers an' his Flyin' X bunch sort o' got on Hewell's nerves."

"Who're you?" inquired Ware, scowling. He did not like this business particularly. "Who's Withers?"

"Me? I'm Bud Childers. My dad was wiped out by that o'n'ry cow thief, Wynn Eggers, an' I'm goin' to git Eggers right, someday, if I have to help him bust out o' the pen first an' then beat him to the draw. I'm pretty fast now, an' I'm practicin' all time. Withers is the biggest cowman in this country, bosses things gen'ral in Yants County. Him an' Dad never hit her off together."

"What's Withers doing to worry Hewell? Thought Hewell was pretty salty himself. Didn't he almost kill Eggers?"

The boy's face twisted contemptuously. He spat. "Yeh . . . damnedest accident ever yuh hear about, too. He called me a liar about it, but I told 'em what I saw that night. Hewell, he sights Eggers comin' into town . . . Eggers was half drunk an' wantin' to show off . . . an' Eggers sights Hewell about the same time. He rammed the rowels into his hoss an' come down on Hewell hell-bent. Hewell turned an' run like an antelope. Eggers let out a wolf howl an' come foggin' it with a six-shooter in each hand, doin' the double roll. An' Hewell shot over his shoulder as he was poppin' between two houses . . . an' down come Eggers."

"You sure?" cautioned Ware, but his thin lips were twitching.

"Shore? I was across the street in the gallery o' our house, tryin' to git a Forty-Five pistol shell out o' Dad's Forty-Four. Man, I'd've buttonholed Eggers myself, hadn't been fer that blame' pistol ca'tridge gittin' into the carbine's magazine."

Ware was staring curiously about the shabby, bare little office. There were windows high up in one outside wall; a barred door led into the jail at one end; the whitewash on the walls was peeling leprously; there were twenty or thirty reward notices pasted up, dating back for three or four years, some of them. An old oak desk, sadly scarred and battered, three cheap kitchen chairs, and a soapbox filled with sand—such was the furniture.

The familiar yellow of a telegram attracted Ware's second glance to the sand box. He moved over mechanically to retrieve the ball of paper. He flattened it out, read absently for the first two words, then was alert attention. He lifted his narrowed eyes to the grim, slim boy of old Sheriff Childers.

"Reckon this is why Hewell high-tailed it. He knew somebody working at the pen?"

"Yeah. Sim. His brother. Guard there."

"Listen to this. 'Watch out. Wynn Eggers and three other life-termers broke out late yesterday. Think they were helped from outside. Horses waiting for them. Eggers may make for Yants County and has many times threatened to kill you.' That's signed Sim, so. . . ."

"If that damn' killer does come down this way"—Bud Childers faced Ware with teeth showing wolfishly—"he'll never go back but feet first! Not if I lay my eyes on him!"

"This thing's a week old," remarked Ware, noting the telegram's date. "Hmm . . . reckon Eggers has had time to get here . . . unless he was caught again . . . and I reckon, if Hewell was so scared of him, he wouldn't have hiked so sudden, if Eggers was back in the pen. Wonder how come he stuck here so long, figuring Eggers was on his way back to this country?"

"Don' know . . . 'less he figured Eggers couldn't git back inside of a week or so. Yuh reckon, Ware, Eggers'd be fool enough to come back this-a-way?"

"They do break for their home country, lots of times. Did he leave friends behind him, around here?"

"Well, they do say that a lot o' the Flyin' X boys used to cow hunt with him. An' me, personal, I wouldn't put nothin' past Bill Withers. I know some things he has done, an' standin' in with a cow thief an' murderer ain't nothin' alongside 'em. My dad, he knowed lots more. That's why him an' Bill didn't git along . . . an' why Bill, he never pined to tangle with Dad."

Came a long, shrill wolf howl from the street a little way off, but Childers grinned, with a certain grimness about his young mouth, a certain speculation in his blue eyes as Ware studied the impassive youngster.

"That's Bill Withers . . . half drunk an' lettin' Yantsboro know who's boss," Childers explained. "He gits that-a-way about onct a month. Well . . . you're actin' sher'ff."

"What does Hewell do about it?" asked Ware, frowning toward the door, through which came stronger, and stronger still, the shrill yells of the cowman boss. "This business of leaving a sheriff's job in my lap doesn't tickle me a bit . . . when there aren't full directions on the bottle."

"Hewell? Hell, he leaves him clean alone," grinned Bud Childers contemptuously. "We got a city marshal, but he's a Flyin' X 'puncher throwed into the job by Bill Withers. Harrel's his name. Lanky fella with a skinny face an' a big nose. He ain't goin' to put the hobbles onto Withers. He ain't even goin' to try it."

"Reckon I'll have to talk to Withers," sighed Ware, slipping down from the end of the desk upon which he had been seated. "He's started cussing, and there's women on the street. Have to ask him to cut it out, I reckon."

"He looks fat, but he's real hard," Bud informed Ware with eyes fixed upon the ceiling. "Left-handed, too. Hits . . . or shoots . . . that-a-way. Hits right sudden, too. He smashed Hewell one time, an' the sher'ff never woke up for half an hour."

Bill Withers had reached the sidewalk on the far side of the street, opposite the sheriff's office, when Ware came out upon the street. It seemed to the ranger that the cowman was not altogether unstudied in his uproar, that Withers was looking at the sheriff's office out of the corner of his eye. He went quietly across the dusty street and cut in ahead of

Withers, who halted as if seeing him for the first time—and as if he were none too favorably impressed by what he saw.

"Mister Withers," said Ware in a friendly tone, "they tell me you're a big man in this country . . . one that everybody looks up to and respects."

"Well?" demanded Withers, his heavy red face uncertain of expression, as if he had expected a different approach. "What's all that to you? Who the hell are you anyhow, a-stoppin' *me* on the street this way?"

"I'm a Texas Ranger . . . and acting sheriff of the county right now. What I'm getting at is there's ladies on the street that can hear you a-cussing, and I wish you wouldn't do it any more. Nobody's trying to stop you or anything like that. But if you'll just remember about the ladies, I know you aren't going to make a row like this, where they can hear you . . . have to hear you."

"Well, if this ain't beatin' hell!" cried Bill Withers, and his great body began visibly to swell. "A blame' li'l squirt like you tellin' me what to do! Well, sir, she shore does beat hell! An' they're takin' the likes o' you in the rangers nowadays! Well, I be eternally damned."

"I've got a hard enough job on my hands, trying to be sheriff of a county I don't know a blame thing about," pleaded Ware, "without the big men . . . like you-all, Mister Withers . . . a-making it harder. Now, won't you think about what I said? Won't you stop your cussing on the street?"

"I'll do as I damn' please!" roared Withers furiously. "I'll cuss if I want to, an' I'll howl if I want to. No blame kid's goin' to tell me nothin'!"

"Maybe I'm just a kid and all," shrugged Ware. "But I'm about as big as I expect to get. And big or not, I'm a Texas Ranger, and the only officer in sight. Now, I'm telling you"— abruptly his voice lost its gentle, deceptive drawling notes and snapped like brittle glass—"if you so much as open your filthy mouth on this street again, I'll slam you into the jail yonder so quick it'll take you a week to sort out your ends, one from another."

Flashingly—for he marked the quivering of Bill Withers's gun hand—a white-handled Colt came out from beneath the goatskin jumper.

"Don't you make no breaks for a gun, either. I'm giving you this last chance. High-tail it and don't look back. If I hear a peep out of you, I'll come for you . . . and if I have to, I'll sure come smoking. Now, get."

"I'll git yo' job for this! I'll pull some strings in Austin that'll heave you out on yore ear! You can't git away with nothin' like this with me! I'll. . . ."

"I've heard all that so many times from Twenty-Two-caliber county bosses that it doesn't worry me half so much as rain on a tin roof," Ware told him wearily. "Get!"

He watched Withers go back up the street, then returned to the sheriff's office. Bud Childers, who had been standing in the doorway, eyed him with dawning of a vast respect. "Yuh fooled me for a li'l bit," he grinned. "They tell some tall stories about yuh, Ware, but I reckon they're mostly so. Now, if yuh want to do somethin' Hewell was always scared to do, yuh'll drag in Pancho Muñoz. He knifed another Mex this mawning, an' he's down in Hogtown. Sent word to Hewell, he did, that if the sher'ff's office wanted him bad enough to come git him, he'd be right pleased to be arrested . . . mebbe."

"Bad Mex, is he?"

"Don' know," shrugged Bud Childers. "Reckon he sort o' knows who to buck up to. Hewell's scared to go down into Hogtown among the Mexicans, I know that."

"Is there a complaint against him for this knifing?"

185

"Shore! I heard the dead man's woman tellin' Hewell about it."

"How'll I know Muñoz?"

"Squatty li'l Mex. Face all scarred up with smallpox. One ear gone. Yuh would know him in a thousand. I'll go along."

"No-o. I've got no right to drag you-all into this. Reckon I'd better go down and see if I can talk Muñoz into coming in."

Bud Childers began to whistle, twirling the ancient cap-and-ball Colt upon a forefinger and smiling at the ceiling. And Ware, frowning at him, sensed a kindred soul and knew that, when he got into Hogtown, there would be some one at his back—someone, he began to believe, more than usually brave, efficient. He shrugged.

"All right, but let me walk in by myself."

In the doorway, Bud Childers pointed inconspicuously at the hawk-faced cowboy whom Ware had first noted in Murfree's store—he who had risen and gone out with the bloated man of purple nose. "That there's Harrel, the city marshal. Looks like he ain't too pleased about somethin', an' I bet yuh I know how come. He just about run into Bill Withers, an' Bill ask' him what he was goin' to do about yuh."

"Harrel set himself up for a gunman?" inquired Ware thoughtfully. It is always well to know what to expect, and the would-be gunman is very often more dangerous than the fellow with credentials notched on his gun butts.

"Kind o' likes hisself," nodded Bud with a grim lip-twitching, as they watched Harrel go on toward the other end of town. "But he ain't actually slung no lead yit. Well, le's go! Now, yuh'll likely find Pancho a-swellin' it around Dogface Chacon's joint. An' as long as a man keeps his back to the wall an' his eyes peeled for a throwed knife, he ain't in much grief at Dogface Chacon's."

* * * * *

Ware attracted vastly less attention in the narrow, crooked ways of Hogtown, the Mexican section of Yantsboro, than he had roused that morning in Murfree's store. For his clothing was that of the correctly clad Mexican dandy; his dark tanned face had more than once in the past caused him to be taken for a Mexican. So now the women wearing *rebosos* and the men wearing sombreros that he passed hardly glanced at him fully, contenting themselves with study of his expensive garb.

Dogface Chacon's *cantina* was a white-plastered adobe with street front at least twice as long as that of any other house in Hogtown. Over the main door was a crude, but vivid, representation of the Mexican flag; to right and left of this six feet wide entrance were other, smaller, doors. Ware had been clicking along carelessly enough, approaching the place. But at the big, dusky entrance, he suddenly was making no more sound than a moccasined Apache. He slid along the wall of the gloomy passageway and stopped where he could look into the great, crowded barroom of the *cantina*. And two men he marked instantly, where they drank together at the far end of a long, unpainted pine bar—Pancho Muñoz, squat, chocolate-brown of skin, with wrinkled scar about his left ear hole and sinister, pockmarked face, and Bill Withers.

On the other side of the bar was an enormous Mexican with greasy black hair and a long, yellowish face amazingly like that of an outlaw broncho—quite obviously Dogface Chacon himself.

Ware waited with eyes beginning to show a greenish war flame. Here was more than he had bargained for when he started out to gather in the Mexican outlaw. What did Bill Withers, Flying X owner and political boss of Yants County, want with such as Pancho Muñoz? Evidently it was something requiring a good deal of explanation on the part of

Withers, for he was talking with great earnestness and much movement of thick, hairy hands. Pancho Muñoz listened with a set frown, nodding vaguely. Dogface Chacon's long, yellow face was immovable as a rock. Suddenly, at something Withers said, Dogface's head jerked a trifle to one side, and he regarded the white man steadily. Pancho Muñoz fairly gaped.

Ware was watching, so he saw Muñoz's lips move and as plainly as coarse print read the ejaculation of the Mexican killer—"The sheriff!"—gasped Muñoz in English. Then he threw back his head and laughed and laughed, until he had to hold on to the bar's edge, and the tears streamed down his pockmarked face. Even Dogface's eyes seemed to hold a glint of amusement, and Withers was grinning widely.

They talked for two or three minutes longer, Pancho listening closely again. Then Withers tossed down the remnant of his drink, shook hands with Pancho, nodded to Dogface, and went waddling down the bar to turn at its end and enter a passage that Ware thought was another exit to the street. And Ware moved inside now.

Somehow he managed to cross the crowded room without rousing suspicion in those he passed, without even attracting the attention of Pancho Muñoz, who leaned with both elbows upon the bar and moved his glass of lemon-colored tequila aimlessly. From his occasional gusts of silent laughter, Pancho was still amused by something. Dogface had disappeared through a door in the thick wall behind the bar, closing it after him. Ware stood at Pancho's elbow before the killer observed him.

"I wish to speak to you, Muñoz . . . outside," Ware told him, speaking softly at the very head of the Mexican, his lips at the earless opening.

Muñoz whirled like a startled cat, one hand flashing to his

waist. Ware stood on his left, his right shoulder drooping like
a cripple's, his right hand held in a stiff, grotesque knot. All
this Muñoz seemed to see in one lightning-swift glance, and,
while his fingers remained hooked in the red sash about his
middle, he made no further move.

"*¿Porque?*" he demanded. "Why do you wish to talk to
me?"

"That will appear," said Ware. "Let us go to the street and
I can tell you in a very few words."

"No," snapped Muñoz. "Whatever you have to say, say
here. I am Pancho Muñoz. I come and go as pleases me. I do
not permit. . . ."

The knotted right hand of Ware opened and down from
the loose sleeve of his jumper slid a Colt, until the curved butt
nestled in his palm, the hammer flipped back, and the muzzle
poked Muñoz in the side.

"You come and go as pleases me," drawled Ware. "Now,
you will go very quietly, making a cigarette . . . very slowly . . .
as you go. You will remember that I am behind you, and, if
you make a suspicious movement, the tiniest sound . . . well,
we shall see."

Sullenly, Muñoz accepted Durham and brown papers.
Draggingly, with head shuttling from left to right as in search
of an avenue of escape, he moved toward the entrance
through which Ware had come. At the end of the bar, opposite the passageway down which Withers had disappeared,
Ware saw a suggestion of stiffening in the killer's back—as in
the body of a runner waiting for the starting signal. And his
right palm, knotted again with the muzzle of the concealed
Colt resting upon it, began to open.

In that moment, in the doorway of that passage, appeared
Bud Childers and his right thumb was hooked in the belt that
held up the ancient, long-barreled, cap-and-ball Colt. He

looked hard at Muñoz, and the killer went on toward the front entrance. Ware quickened his pace and was immediately behind him when Muñoz entered the dusky passage. Bud Childers came lounging after.

"Un momento," snapped Ware—and Muñoz halted. "No. Lift those hands. Lift them before I shoot. Go through him, Bud . . . and don't you leave him so much as a toothpick."

"Reg'lar arsenal, he is," grinned Bud, when he held out a pair of beautiful .38 Colts, two heavy throwing knives, and a slender dagger. "I g'arantee he ain't packin' nothin' else. Well?"

"Reckon you can just hang onto those sixes," returned Ware. "If they don't hang Pancho, and he ever comes after 'em. . . ."

"I'll hand 'em over, all right . . . muzzle first."

"OK, Muñoz," snapped Ware. "You will walk straight to the sheriff's office and go inside. We will be one ahead and one behind you . . . in order that such good resolutions as you are making now may not turn sour. *¡Andar!"*

And so it was done. Through Hogtown they went, and Ware was thinking more of the conversation he had seen between this Mexican killer and Yants County's political boss than of the sullen figure ahead of him. His thoughts came abruptly back to Muñoz, however, when the Mexican suddenly stopped on the edge of the American part of town and set himself like a balky mule.

"I will go no farther!" proclaimed Muñoz. "You dare not injure me, for I am charged with no crime that anyone witnessed . . . that anyone who will talk witnessed. You are not an officer of this county. You. . . ."

Ware hit him scientifically upon the chin, and Muñoz sprawled limply in the dust. Ware waited, but Muñoz's eyes were closed. A harsh voice spoke in Ware's ear.

"Cut that out! Where the hell d'yuh think yuh are, hittin' citizens o' this town? I'm city marshal, an' I'd just as soon slam yuh into jail as. . . ."

Ware turned slowly to face Harrel, the ex-Flying X 'puncher. Harrel's hawk-face was a mirror of outraged dignity. He was waggling a forefinger at Ware.

"And a fine city marshal you turned out to be," sneered Ware. "Scared to pull in Bill Withers for disturbing the peace . . . scared to death to go down into Hogtown after a common, ornery, yellow-livered Mexican killer."

"Looky yere!" roared Harrel. "I don't have to take no talk offen yuh! I'm city marshal, an' I'm runnin' things to suit myself. By God, I'll just take yuh to the calaboose an'. . . ."

His hand went toward the butt of his right-hand gun—for he packed two, the muzzles of his holsters held to his boot tops by fancy horsehair cords. Ware made no motion toward the now holstered sixes under his jumper. Instead, he took one flashing step forward, and, exactly as he had smashed Muñoz, a hard fist came up in a swinging overhand right to loosen the marshal's front teeth. Harrel went sprawling, with empty hands falling loosely to his sides.

Ware bent over and twitched the Colts from Harrel's holsters. Then he stood prodding him with boot toe, while the grinning Bud Childers stood guard upon Pancho Muñoz until Harrel groaned and opened his eyes.

"Get up," commanded Ware. "On your feet, you four-flushing imitation of a badman. You know damn' well I'm a Texas Ranger, and I'm telling you here and now . . . don't you bother me. Here! You don't look bad to me. Here's your guns. Start smoking or not, as you like. Don't want any, huh? All right. On your way . . . and don't look back." Then, as Harrell went up the street as he had been told to do, Ware drawled grimly to Bud: "I sure do smell something behind all this. That windbag never locked horns with me on his own hook. And this *hombre* on the ground . . . who's going to git up and come along real sweet right now . . . he was listening to some scheme of Bill Withers's back in Dogface Chacon's Mexican Flag place. Let's go. Reckon the only way to brand is to take 'em calf by calf."

They put Pancho Muñoz into the single big cell of the jail, but shackled him to the great cottonwood log set into the adobe wall. It was late afternoon. Ware had eaten nothing since the breakfast he had cooked on the trail. Childers went out to a Chinese restaurant and brought in a meal for each of them. Between mouthfuls, Bud talked—of the country that he knew intimately and of his two ambitions: to kill Wynn Eggers and to join the Texas Rangers.

"Try to help you get in," nodded Ware half absently. "I was about your size when I joined. You look to me like the right kind of timber. We'll see. Right now, I'm wondering what Bill Withers is figuring. I'd give a month's pay to find out. *The sheriff!* That was what Pancho Muñoz said in the *cantina* . . . then he like to died laughing. Withers went on and told him a long rigmarole about something."

"Funny," nodded Bud Childers. "Bill Withers and Pancho . . . they might be up to just about anything yuh could figure. Mebbe Withers was tellin' how Hewell skipped out so sudden."

Childers was staring through the door, and suddenly he straightened up, the better to look. Ware's black brows climbed, and he, too, glanced through the doorway. It meant nothing to him—the sight of two cowboys staggering along the opposite side of the street, arm in arm, apparently dead drunk—but Bud Childers was shaking his head slightly, frowning.

"There's that useless Ike Simpkins o' Withers's Flyin' X, hobnobbin' with Shorty Roberts . . . Hewell's 'puncher."

"Meaning?"

"Meanin' nothin' to me, personal, but a heap to Shorty. Hewell will hand him his time the minute he finds out."

"For hanging out with a Flying X man?"

"Nah. Because there ain't nobody on Hewell's place with Shorty in town. An' Hewell thinks as much o' them three full-blood hosses o' his an' that half-blood as most men think about their wives an' kids. He ain't got a big place, nor many head o' stuff, but they're all fine, an' we're too close to the river to leave that kind o' stock alone. Ben Burrus is in town here, sick. So Shorty's s'posed to stick on the place." He shrugged and turned back from the door. "Well, she ain't no funereal o' mine, but wouldn't this be the great time to run off Hewell's stuff? Not a peace officer in the county, an' nobody but you to watch?"

"I wonder?" grinned Ware abruptly, staring at Bud Childers. "I . . . wonder. Bud! Go snoop around and see what Withers and his outfit are doing . . . and what that four-flushing marshal is up to. Get back as soon as you find out what there is to find out. I've got a feeling that this is likely to be a busy night for us."

As Ware sat smiling to himself in the growing dusk of the office, waiting for the action he felt in his bones must come, presently footsteps sounded outside. A Mexican appeared in the doorway and came through, staggering. Harrel's figure showed for an instant behind him.

"Drunk Mex," grunted Harrel. "Heave him into the lock-up, will yuh, Ranger? See yuh after while."

Ware slid down from the desk end and moved toward the Mexican, who stood swaying with teeth showing whitely against his brown face in a foolish grin.

"Come along," said Ware.

He was within three feet of the swaying figure when the Mexican straightened and leaped straight at him. A knife flashed in each hand. Instinctively, Ware ducked and sensed one blade going over his shoulder. The other point struck him heavily upon the breast, then he had the Mexican by the throat and was flinging him sideways. He kicked him in the chin, and the fellow groaned, kicked him again and saw him go limp. Then he got the knives.

Only the way he carried his Colts had saved him from a serious wound. The point of the knife had struck the cylinder of a six-shooter and had hung in the heavy leather of the holster. Beyond a nick a quarter inch deep he was unhurt. He was bending over the dazed Mexican, about to haul him up and shackle him beside Muñoz, when a sudden thought came. He turned it over, grinned a little to himself.

There was a lariat on the wall. He got it and bound the Mexican with turn after turn and knots that would hardly be unloosed by the prisoner. Finally he gagged the captive, and then he dragged him awkwardly out through the door that led into a passageway to the rear of the building. He put the Mexican in a corner of the corral and came back at a panting trot.

"Ware?" came an anxious call from the dusky office, and he answered.

"Thought somethin' mebbe had happened," said Bud Childers in relief. "Don' know what's happenin', but two Flyin' X boys an' Shorty Roberts is drunker'n five hundred dollars in the Last Chanct, an' Bill Withers an' his range boss an' Harrel . . . they're thicker'n thieves at t'other end o' the bar."

"I see . . . heaps, maybe. Now, Bud, you hike back up the street. Who's the doctor here?"

"Fella named Atkins. Ain't been here long. Young fella. Lives about four houses from here."

"Fine. Reckon he's home?"

"He was settin' on the gallery when I come by."

"All right. I'm going up to his place . . . from the back. I'll put the jail keys right here in the middle of the floor. Now, you get back to the Last Chance and tell that gang that you found me dying from stab wounds in the office, an' that I'm lying up at Doc Atkins's house. Get real worked about it, Bud. Maybe I'm wrong, but . . . maybe I'm governor of Texas, too. Come back to Atkins's soon as you can slip off."

Waiting in the doctor's office, Ware heard the clumping of many feet in the gallery of the house. He winked at young Dr. Atkins who grinned in reply, then sobered abruptly, and went outside.

"You never know how a wound of this sort will turn out," Ware caught the doctor's solemn pronouncement. "It's always difficult to gauge the exact depth." This was followed by a good deal of impressive technical verbiage.

"Must've been that Mex I asked him to slam into the lock-up," came Harrel's voice. "I told the ranger, though, that I hadn't no chanct to search the Mex. Told him he better see what the fella had on him. It's shore too bad."

"Well, they're gone," shrugged the doctor, coming back.

"Thanks a heap, Doc," grinned Ware. "I reckon maybe you've done a good job for your country tonight. Can't tell you no more right now, for I don't know a lot myself. I'll be high-tailing it."

He slipped out to the back and waited for Bud Childers. The boy appeared in a moment, running silently on high boot heels.

"They let Pancho Muñoz out o' jail. They're all laughin'

an' tellin' Harrel what a talent he's got for lyin'. They all rode out o' town, headin' west . . . an' that ain't the way to the Flyin' X, neither."

"No, but I'll bet it's the way to Hewell's place," Ware speculated.

"Yuh mean . . . ?" breathed Bud Childers. "I bet yuh you're right."

"Listen. Is Shorty Roberts still being shepherded around by the Flying X?"

"Reckon. Bill Withers, Harrel, Pancho Muñoz, Sully, Withers's range boss, and another fella I couldn't make out was all that rode off?"

"Five, huh? Can we beat 'em to the Hewell place?"

"If we git off the road an' ride like hell," said Bud simply. "They didn't act like they was in a big sweat."

"They'll be in a real big sweat when we start the ball rolling," Ware promised grimly. "What's Pancho in this deal? Reckon he's to handle the horses on the Mexican side?"

"That's what I figure. Lots o' folks suspicion that Pancho's got a gang that works from old Mexico."

Childers seemed to know the Hewell place intimately, even in the darkness. There was a gate in the south fence of the horse pasture through which, he said with conviction, the stolen animals would be driven. Hewell's house loomed, dark and silent, in a smaller pasture above the main enclosure. Ware and Bud took up position in the rear of the house, reining in their animals close to the wall.

There was not ten minutes to wait. The oncoming riders acted as if this were a pleasure trip. They were laughing and talking loudly as they rode up to the house.

"We'll help you round 'em up, Pancho!" Bill Withers announced in a voice that might have been heard halfway to

Yantsboro. "Man, this shore's goin' to be a joke on Hewell. Pancho, he busts jail an' takes the sher'ff's pet ponies along with him! Reckon there's anything in the house worth takin' along? Got to make her look like a bunch o' raidin' Mexes, you know."

"Nah!" cried Harrel contemptuously. "Hewell don't believe in puttin' nothin' into the shack. Better git the goats started fer that south gate. Come on!"

"I'm goin to see!" chuckled Withers. "You all go on."

He rode around the house, and his horse all but cannoned into Rocket, Ware's black stallion. An instant later Ware had Withers's bridle reins at the bits and was staring down at the big, moveless figure on the ground. At that moment another rider came in Withers's wake, riding carelessly, with hands cupped about the flame of the match with which he lit his cigarette.

Bud Childers gasped audibly, and the rider laughed harshly.

"Don't be so jumpy, Bill. It's me . . . Eggers. Thought. . . ."

"Stick up yore paws, yuh damn' murderer!" cried Bud Childers thinly.

There was a confusion of movement—the boy's gun flashing, Eggers's horse rearing and staggering into Withers's mount, jerking the reins from Ware's hand. Then Eggers's animal whirled around the corner of the house and was gone at a gallop.

"I'll git him if I have to tail him a thousand miles," snarled Bud Childers, and was off in a flash.

Ware left Withers and spurred toward the big pasture. Calls were coming from Harrel and the range boss; they wanted to know the meaning of the shot and the sound of galloping hoofs.

"It's me . . . Eggers!" yelled Ware huskily. Then he laughed. "Rode up behind Bill an' scared him. He shot an' his hoss ran off with him!"

They laughed, and Ware came on toward them. Presently he could make out their figures—blobs of darkness against the night.

"Pancho says he don't need no help," said Harrel. "He's done so much o' this he can work blindfold."

"Got nothin' on the Flyin' X," chuckled the range boss. "Bill Withers could start a school an' learn Chinks how to make ever' cow come through with twelve calves a season!"

Ware sat just behind them with a Colt in each hand. He was listening strainedly, and presently he caught the sound he sought, hoofbeats returning. Closer and closer. It would be Bud Childers or—Wynn Eggers. He drew a long, slow breath. In a couple of minutes he might have to kill three men. Closer came the hoofs; up to the house they were now.

"Bill's comin' back," grunted Harrel. "He's stopped at the house."

"Just reach up, Harrel . . . an' your friend'll do likewise . . . and grab hold of your ears," invited Ware levelly. "I've got a gun on each of you, and I'm not missing at three feet."

"I . . . I . . . ," gasped Harrel.

"You thought I was kicking off?" mocked Ware. "Well, I'm real pert, thanks! Got a good dally on them ears? All right! Bud! Bud Childers! Come on up!"

Painfully, indeed, he waited. If that were Wynn Eggers . . . ? But it was Bud, and he drew rein short and slid his horse to a halt.

"Take these jaspers' guns and then cuff 'em. I've got a half dozen pair of cuffs in my saddlebags. Got 'em? Good enough. Now, you want to watch these imitation horse thieves while I go gather in Pancho again?"

"Let me! Yuh already collected him onct, an' I ain't done a thing. Missed that damn' Eggers, an' his hoss dragged him to death."

He was gone into the shadows before Ware could object. There were long minutes to wait, then a faraway yell. Hoofbeats came in slow time, then Bud Childers's shrill, boyish voice. "He's a reg'lar li'l lamb, Pancho is. Minute he heard yuh wanted him to come on up an' quit botherin' Hewell's hosses, he says . . . shore!"

Two hours later, with the lock-up of the caboose crammed with their prisoners, with the body of Wynn Eggers in Dr. Atkins's office, with the drunken Shorty Roberts snoring against the wall of the sheriff's office, Ware looked thoughtfully at Bud Childers.

"Fella," he said, "I'm sure going to take you back to Cap'n Knowles and tell him you're the pure quill. And I figure he'll take you in. Of course, we'll have to be witnesses against Bill Withers and the rest, but that won't take long, I reckon."

"And yuh telegraphed Hewell he's safe to leave his kid in the hospital," grinned Bud, cuddling the two .38s "donated" by Pancho Muñoz. "Well, what's next?"

"Nothing now," said Ware. He stretched luxuriously. "Call it a day."

Spiderweb Trail

The stage road was not nearly so much of a road as the term implied. The road-builders had graded steep arroyo banks to permit vehicles to cross; they had hacked out rude shelves around the shoulders of the hills; they had blasted boulders from the right of way where it was utterly impossible to go around. But this was all. Still, to a horseman, the stage road leading eastward to Monitor and the little towns beyond offered a quite passable route.

Ware, who was officially designated a second sergeant in the Texas Rangers, found the road both average by Western standards and—interesting. For on this road it was that the westbound stage, coming through Monitor from the mines, had five times been held up with a precision, an efficiency, a mystery that utterly baffled the sheriff of Picacho County.

Writing to Ware's captain to ask for a ranger, Sheriff Robey had remarked upon a certain uniformity noted about these robberies—each time the trails of two horses had been noted leading to the scene of the hold-up. Clear to the edge of Monitor the officer had back-tracked these hoof prints. But always they were lost in the town's main street amid a confusion of other tracks. Always, too, there was no indication of their return to town by any traceable course.

"Looks kind of like the sheriff's harboring the robbers and not able to help himself," Ware had remarked in the captain's tent, finishing Sheriff Robey's letter. "And, Monitor being a right smart town these days, checking up on everybody isn't the easiest job a fella could handle before breakfast."

"Does look like a pretty tough nut to crack," the captain had agreed. "What Robey says about the robbers leaving the stage alone when it carried extra shotgun men makes it look like they know what's going on. If they can't slip in guards without the robbers knowing it beforehand, then the robbers are on the inside track."

Ware slouched in the big, silver-rimmed saddle and whistled softly between his teeth. He was perfectly happy as he jogged toward the new job. There were men in the wide and sovereign State of Texas who regarded him as something more—or less—than human, men who had crossed his trail or feared that he would cross theirs. They regarded him as a sort of machine operated by the state for the unraveling of mysteries, the detection of crime. A slim, smallish figure in wide-brimmed Mexican sombrero and short *charro* jacket of soft-tanned goatskin, he held a larger place in outlaws' imaginations than many a more ferocious, but more usual, peace officer.

Monitor must be right over the hill, he thought suddenly, staring ahead along the run of the rugged, green-brown Sentinels that walled in the right-hand side of the stage road. *So it can't be far from here where the stage is always stuck up.*

He tickled Rocket's flank affectionately with a star-rowel, and the big stallion shook his head. It was only pleasantly warm, although the time was noon and the month July. Over the peaks of the Sentinels—and across the length of the Monitors twenty miles over the flats on the left—thunderstorms hovered, joining, separating, joining again, in masses of dusky, blue-black clouds. Not a drop of rain fell on the road, though.

"Come on, old-timer," Ware admonished the stallion aloud. "You ol' sugar-beggar, you. Rattle them hocks or one of these days I'll swap you even-steven for a burro!"

There was a strong affection between stallion and rider, remarkable in a land where men took their horses pretty much for granted as a means of transportation—something to be ridden hard and discarded for new mounts whenever necessary. But Rocket was an educated animal. He would break down a door to answer Ware's whistle; he would drop flat and lie still at a double whistle; he would do a half-dozen things that no other horse would do. Ware was vastly proud of him.

So now, as they approached a ten-foot cutbank, where the road had been hacked out of a mountain shoulder above a deep cañon, Rocket slipped from running-walk to fox-trot while Ware drew from jacket pocket the Durham and the brown papers and began to make a cigarette. Sounded, now, a tiny rustling on the greasewood-studded crest of the cutbank. Ware, habitually alert as a wild animal, ceased shaking tobacco into paper and started to lift his head. But a snaky coil fell about his neck and drew taut before his chin had raised an inch.

Instinctively he knew what had happened. Tobacco and paper went flying. His hands shot up, but the loop of the lariat had tightened about his throat. His mouth sagged open, his eyes bulged, and he came draggingly out of the saddle. Rocket, startled, surged ahead, and Ware crashed to earth. The universe rolled and heaved like a sea before his popping eyes; then it seemed to explode noiselessly in whirl after whirl of spinning countless miles through flame-shot space into fathomless darkness. For an instant there penetrated to him the sound of someone laughing, an eerie, mocking sound. But he was conscious of this for but a split second. After that, he was conscious of nothing.

The sun beating down into his face roused him. He

opened his eyes and blinked stupidly upward. The slanting sunlight came over a low arroyo bank and directly onto him. He tried to roll over, and then it was that he found himself bound hands and feet. His mouth was dry; when he tried to swallow, his throat throbbed agonizingly. Slowly he recalled everything; the swelling in his throat reminded him of the lariat that had dragged him from the saddle.

After several efforts he could sit up and stare around him. He had been lying in a shallow arroyo, from which he could not see the stage road. All was silent around him, and he refrained from making any noise. Instead, he cocked a calculating eye at the sun and decided that three hours, at least, had passed since his loss of consciousness. This puzzled him. How had he come to lie senseless so long? His head ached, throbbing dully. Perhaps, he thought, he had landed upon it, then remembered that he had not. He began to work his hands—lashed together at the wrists behind him. He curved his fingers and found the knots and picked with fingertips.

Time passed, but finally he was able to slip his wrists from the loops. Then it was that he saw that he had been bound with his own fine rawhide lariat, rather with lengths cut from it. To free his bootless feet was the work of two minutes; then he rested. Neither hat, boots, nor *charro* jacket was in sight. He pursed his thin lips to whistle for Rocket then shook his head. It might not be safe. The white-handled Colts were gone from his holsters. He put his hand to his head and screwed up his face at the touch, then probed carefully.

It was not hard to understand his long time of unconsciousness. There was a gash in his scalp six inches long, over which the blood had matted his dark hair. Ware's lean, brown face set in an emotionless mask more threatening than would have been unchecked fury. His captor, not content with choking him senseless, had very evidently cracked him over the head with a .45 barrel to make sure of him. Then he had mysteriously plundered him of everything on his person— even to Durham, matches, and the book of brown papers!

Ware went down the arroyo in the direction of the stage road without more noise than a crawling rattler might have made. In his hand he gripped a smooth stone that might have weighed a pound, for he was as primitively bent upon killing, in that moment, as any Neolithic forebear he might have had. But when he wriggled out of the arroyo and looked down upon the dusty floor of the road, there was no trace anywhere of life. He hesitated momentarily, then whistled Rocket's call.

No answer. Again and again he whistled and listened strainedly. Then he was assured that Rocket was beyond hearing. So he descended to the road, moving carefully among yucca and prickly pear and knife-edged stone in socked feet. It was not hard to pick up the trail he had made coming beneath the crest of the low bluff upon which his captor had lain in hiding. There were the familiar prints of Rocket's hoofs ending in a flurry of dust. There was the long sliding track where Ware had sprawled at the end of the lariat.

He moved cautiously forward, stooping to study the road's surface. The tracks of Rocket had been overlaid by wheel prints and the hoof marks of little Spanish mules. At the end of the cut nearest Monitor was the place where the stage had been stopped. Ware moved like an Apache about this spot. And just beyond it he picked up in the midst of the mules' tracks the trail of two horses, coming from Monitor. As Sheriff Robey had written, the stage robberies were always accompanied by this outward-bound trail, and this robbery of today had been uniform with the others.

Scouting in circles, Ware found Rocket's trail again. It led down the road a little way toward Monitor, then turned away, up a little ridge. And beside it Ware found, pointing from the general direction of Monitor toward the scene of the robbery, the tracks of one of the horses whose trail had joined with another to make the regular two-man robbers' trail the sheriff had always found. Ware decided that he was in no condition to go farther. He needed boots and weapons and a horse. Then. . . .

"It'll be a long-legged gunny that pulls a job like this and gets away," he remarked aloud in flat Texas drawl. "Fellas, if you-all got anything to do, you sure better get it over with. For when I come up with you, I'm going to do my blamedest to hand you the trouble you ordered."

He went back to the road and started toward Monitor. After a couple miles he began to limp a little, and by the time he had covered ten miles—this was in the twilight—and saw the rambling spread of Monitor in a small valley below him, he was limping in earnest. He came through the edge of town and stopped in the shadows beside a store, to look down the main street. A Mexican boy came by.

"*Muchacho,*" said Ware, in Spanish. "Where is the office of *Señor* the Sheriff?"

The boy pointed to a square adobe down the street, but volunteered the information that the sheriff was just then at home, eating supper.

"I will go on to the office," said Ware in Spanish. "Will you go to the sheriff and say that one awaits him in his office on business of urgency. Ask him to come there as soon as he has eaten."

"*Sí, señor,*" nodded the boy, staring curiously at this smallish, extremely disheveled figure who spoke so grimly from the shadows. He started at a trot.

"*Un momento,*" called Ware, and the youngster came

back. Then: "Have you a cigarette upon you? *¡Gracias!* A match? *Mil gracias.* Come you back with the sheriff and I will pay you for doing this commission for me."

And with the cornshuck cigarette glowing, he went toward the sheriff's office. It was open and dark. Ware found a chair with seat of laced rawhide thongs and made himself inconspicuously comfortable in a corner. The minutes ticked off until a half hour had passed. Evidently, he thought, the sheriff was not one to miss a meal because of a summons. But finally he heard the scuff of high heels upon the dirt sidewalk. He rose and came to the door.

"Sheriff?" he inquired. "I'm Ware, Texas Ranger. Give that boy a half dollar for me, will you? Then come on inside and shut the door."

The sheriff grunted something to himself, but fished out the coin and came in. He closed the door behind him, groped across to a kerosene lamp, and scratched a match. Then he turned slowly and at sight of Ware unostentatiously hooked a thumb in his cartridge belt—about two inches from the curving butt of his Colt. His small blue eyes narrowed, half speculatively, half suspiciously. "You're . . . Bill Ware's kid?" he said slowly, and his tone made it seem that he was accusing someone of a lie. "A . . . Texas Ranger . . . ?"

"Stage was robbed today, wasn't it?" Ware remarked quietly. "Thought so," he nodded, reading the sheriff's face. "Well . . . so was I. Complete. Roped out of the saddle by somebody lying on top the cutbank right where the stage was stopped. Choked and smacked over the nut with a six-shooter barrel. Horse and saddle, guns, boots, sombrero, and jacket taken. Had to walk to town. Oh, I'm a Ware, all right. You wrote the cap'n asking for a ranger, and he sent me. And today, when I scouted around the place the stage was robbed, I found the tracks of the two horses coming out of

Monitor toward the place, like you said you always found after a robbery."

The sheriff's suspicious expression vanished with quotation of his letter, and in its stead came sardonic amusement. Suddenly he lifted his gun hand and clapped it against his well-rounded stomach—he was a stocky and well-fed figure, Sheriff Robey. He began to laugh, and from spasmodic giggling his amusement took him to a bellowing like a bull's. At last he controlled himself and stared at the expressionless Ware with eyes from which the tears streamed.

"My . . . stars!" he wheezed. "The ranger that was going to clean up these robbers for me gits hisself roped an' hawg-tied an' robbed hisself! Boy, I've heerd o' you a time or two, an' I thought you had a kind o' reputation. You must've got it kind o' accidental-like, way Bill Moriarty got his rep' for bein' a gunman. Bill, he steps out o' some saloon in Tucson onct, an', bein' half drunk, he blazes away at a tin cup he sees in a window across the street. But he shoots to the left an' kills Toughnut Gorman, who happens to be holdin' the cup. So Bill, he gits a name for killin' Toughnut."

"Much taken today in the robbery?" inquired Ware with blank, set face, only the greenish glow in his eyes to betray his anger.

"Nothin' but what they took off a minin' man from over back. He had three thousand on him, an' he tried to make a fight. They drilled him. Then they hustled the stage on, an' the driver took it into Egan, up the road. We got the word through the railroad agent at Picacho Station. It'd been relayed from Egan there. No wire in Monitor, you know."

"What'd you do about the robbery?" asked Ware. "Send a posse out?"

"No, I never!" the sheriff shrugged, turning red. "What's

the use? I been over the ground forty times, I reckon, after them other robberies. Nothin' different in any o' the five. Too, I been expectin' you to come in, an' I figgered mebbe you'd think o' somethin'. Somethin' new. Oh! This minin' man was shot through the lungs, never killed him, the telegram says."

"Can you fix me up with a horse and saddle and some guns? And loan me enough to get some boots and a hat?"

"Shore. Cal Emerson . . . my deputy . . . he's tryin' to figger out whether to die or not over a gunshot the damn' fool got last week when he went after some Mex. He's about yore size, an' I reckon even his boots'd fit you, till you can git some more made. As for money . . . you can have what you need, o' course."

Ware picked up a piece of brown wrapping paper from the floor and with the stub of a pencil found in his trousers pocket roughly indicated the stage road from Egan to Monitor. Then he pushed it over to the sheriff. "Fill in the map for me, will you?" he asked. "I want to know what the lay of the country is. What's to the north, toward the railroad? South of the Sentinels?"

"Straight north o' town's Henderson's Lazy Z outfit, cattle an' a few good hosses. Southeast o' the Lazy Z . . . that's northeast o' Monitor an' nearer the railroad . . . is Bat Collyer's Open A hoss ranch. Back south o' the Sentinels is the Box U . . . cattle again, ol' Wolf Williams's outfit that's been here forty years. South o' Monitor, then, is the T-Quarter Circle hoss ranch. Hell Creek Hibbs runs it. It and the Box U are both on Hell Creek."

"Good people, all?"

"Like hell!" responded the sheriff simply and earnestly. "The saltiest bunch ever yuh hear about! Ol' Wolf Williams is honest, I reckon, but he shore does just like he pleases. The

211

others . . . well, big an' little, owners an' help, they're hardcases."

"Then," said Ware, "if these robbers of yours hang out in Monitor till time to stick up the stage but don't come straight back to town after, they're maybe hanging out with one of these outfits around . . . anyone but the Box U?"

"You said it . . . the reason I been gittin' gray on this sher'ff's job! They're mebbe hangin' out with *any* o' them outfits. Wolf Williams don't like me a li'l bit, an', as long's them robbers don't bother him none, he don't give a whoop how much they stuck up a stage. He nor his boys'd unload. She's shore got me hornswoggled. I was hopin' a lot I could git a ranger down here that'd see what I can't see, one that'd hang the deadwood onto these robbers."

His mournful use of the past tense showed plainly his poor opinion of the ranger he had got, and Ware smiled grimly. "Election that close?" he asked with sarcasm.

"Next month," growled Robey, then flushed at having his mind read.

"Well, give me something to eat. I'll sleep here, if that's all right with you. Tomorrow . . . where'll I find this deputy's outfit?"

"His hoss is in the corral out back. Saddle's in the shed. I'll send his gun an' boots an' hat down to you t'night. Well, see you some more. Got to go back home, now."

To write letters, I bet, Ware said to himself, watching the sheriff's bulky figure vanish in the darkness. *One to the captain, too . . . telling him all about what happened to me. Well, prayer meeting isn't ever over till the preacher goes home, they say! Maybe we'll have a couple robber-hides drying on the back fence yet.*

Ware was gone from town in the gray of dawn for he feared

that Robey might want to go with him. He had eaten at the same Chinese restaurant that had furnished his supper the night before and carried with him in the deputy's saddlebags bread and cold, fried steak enough to last a couple of days, if necessary. The tall roan of the deputy's was a good enough horse, but he found scant favor in the eyes of Ware, who compared him with the vanished Rocket to his vast disparagement. But he served to bring Ware to that spot where Rocket's trail left the road.

Now Ware whirled the roan up the little ridge. There were the two sets of hoof prints—Rocket's, pointing vaguely to north and east, off toward the Lazy Z or the Open A outfits, and those of the stage robbers, pointing toward the scene of the robbery. Ware rode on slowly, bending from the saddle to trail the stallion. Together, the twin sets of tracks went skirting the foothills of the Monitor Mountains. Now in the bed of an arroyo they showed clearly as if in ashes. On cacti-studded, stony slopes Ware had to dismount and search for the glancing track of an iron shoe upon limestone rocks. Suddenly, after five or six miles of trailing, he drew up with a jerk.

A third trail had come to join these others. A big horse and a heavy one, if he might trust the size and the depths of the impressions. Rocket had halted here before this newcomer—who had come riding down from the northeast. Then the third and newest trail had reversed itself, Rocket accompanying. Ware pushed the mount forward and loosened the carbine a little in the scabbard beneath the fender. He was leaving behind him the trail that led *toward* the robbery.

For five or six miles he managed to follow, then came a long stretch of bare and stony ground upon which no hoof prints showed. He circled for an hour or more, without picking up the trail again. Then he shrugged. He could go on to the two ranches up ahead and look things over, or he could go back to town. It seemed useless at this moment to try the ranches. If Rocket had been taken to one of them, then certainly he would not be left out in view of anyone who came riding up.

As he went back to Monitor, Ware deduced that two robbers had set out from town together, but one had left the road and rejoined his fellow at the scene of the robbery. After capturing Rocket, one had evidently ridden the stallion while the other had doubtless ridden his own horse and led the discarded mount of his companion—led it toward whatever rendezvous they had decided upon.

He found the sheriff in his office, long of face. Very briefly, Ware told Robey of visiting the place where the stage was robbed. The sheriff listened absently, Ware thought. He told Ware that the mining man had died in Egan of his wound. Now came a man to the doorway, a tall man very dandified of clothing, for all that he wore the broad-brimmed Stetson, the blue flannel shirt, jeans trousers, and high-heeled boots of the cow country.

Ware studied this newcomer with habitual intentness, disliking upon first glance the coarsely handsome face with its low, wide forehead, insolent, heavy-lidded green eyes, and Negroid-loose lips. But the sheriff grinned in friendly fashion and lifted a hand.

"Come on in out o' the sun, Tommy," he invited the tall man. "Ware, I want you to meet up with one o' our leadin' citizens, Dan Thomason. Tommy's a freight contractor."

Ware nodded slightly as the freighter loafed inside. Thomason regarded him, a supercilious glint in his green eyes, as he perched himself upon a corner of a desk. He seemed to find sight of Ware's too-large, borrowed boots and shapeless old Stetson highly amusing.

"Heard what you were telling Robey," drawled Thomason. "You found the trail of the highway pair leading out of town and toward the robbery, you said. Well, that's something, of course. But . . . Robey wrote that much to your captain, I recall. You see"—again the amused, superior grin—"we've known that all along."

"Yeah, I gathered you-all knew . . . that much," nodded Ware, narrowed, inscrutable eyes upon the freighter. "The reason the cap'n sent me up to look things over was because you-all didn't know anything else . . . or seem to stand much show of finding out."

"You do, of course," grinned Thomason, with an assumption of tolerance. "Too bad this investigation cost you so much . . . horse, saddle, guns, even your hat and coat, I understand. Seems to me that the ranger appropriation ought to have a provision in it to cover reimbursement for losses like that . . . lariat losses, they might be called."

His long body shook with his amusement. Ware ostentatiously turned away from this unpleasant leading citizen of Monitor and back to Sheriff Robey, who was listening with somewhat uncomfortable expression. "These horse ranches you told me about yesterday," said Ware. "Any of 'em do what you might call small trading?"

"Why, a man might buy or sell or trade a hoss at any of 'em." Robey frowned thoughtfully. "An' I reckon there's hoss-traders hither an' yonder around the country. But namin' one off hand, or tellin yuh where any was yeste'day or day before, is more'n I could do now."

"Well, reckon I'll wander around a spell," shrugged Ware, getting up to move toward the door.

"Best thing," nodded Thomason. "Black stallions aren't so common around the Monitor country that you wouldn't know yours if someone were to ride into town on him. And you ought to recognize your saddle, too. Tell you what, Ranger, that line of hitch racks in front of the Silver Dollar Saloon is the one most used. Better take a look there and see if your stallion's been tied to it. Oh! If you find the fellow who has your horse, what steps will you take?"

Ware turned slowly in the doorway with brown face blank. This was not the first occasion on which he, as a ranger, had met suspicion, unfriendliness, even downright contempt from the peace officers and the citizens of a town. It was merely that this mouthy freighter had more and smoother English in which to phrase his smart-aleck comments. The thought came to Ware, as he looked thoughtfully upon Thomason, that in every instance, heretofore, someone had been forced to a diet of very dusky crow before his, Ware's, departure from the vicinity.

"Why," he made careful answer to Thomason's mockery, "I'm not like a private citizen in a business like this. Ranger has to be mighty careful to keep inside the law and its processes, you know. So, if I find a fella riding Rocket, I'll have to bring him before one of your county officials, regular-like."

"We've one of the finest old justices of the peace in Texas," volunteered Thomason with mock-serious expression. "Shall I ask Judge Beck to be waiting for you?"

"No-o," drawled Ware. "I reckon not. The official I'll bring *my* robber before will be the . . . coroner."

Wandering about the town, Ware was alert not only for the faintest sign and token of that for which he searched—a clue leading to Rocket's present whereabouts—but also he sought for the source of Thomason's importance. Evidently the freight contractor's education had given him the leadership so coveted, in many a small community, by just such pettily egotistical minds. The more Ware walked and looked and listened, the more it became obvious to him that Thomason's position in Monitor was due chiefly to his forward-pushing activities. As a freighter he had no such volume of business as would justify his claim to leadership. A surly, pockmarked old-timer who rejoiced in the illuminating name of Sancho McDougall had the freight business of the whole region in his hard, gnarled old hands. Thomason was the interloper, but not one to worry McDougall in the least. For Sancho had a reputation in all Monitor country and the old-timers swore by him. No—Ware decided—Thomason was not much of a muchness.

He stayed away from Robey's office, wandering here and there, in and out of saloons and dance halls and gambling rooms. In the gallery of Monitor's principal hotel, a big, two-storied adobe, he sat down at last to think. Two men were at the far end of the big, shaded gallery, one sitting sourly with feet cocked up on the rail, the other leaning against a thick adobe post. This latter man, Ware observed idly, seemed in good humor proportionate to his companion's surliness. "Tell you what, Vickery," said the good-humored one, "if I should happen onto anything loose down the line . . . anything my firm don't want to bother with, you know . . . I'll pass the word up to you. It's hell," he went on in tones of deepest sympathy, "just to sit around an' wear out the seat o' your britches. So if I do run onto any li'l deal you could swing, I'll be more'n glad to give you a lift. S'long!"

The sitting man stared grimly straight ahead, keeping his lips tight as against a bitter speech. The sympathetic man moved off, and, as he passed Ware, his happy grin was very obvious. Ware watched the other man sidelong, saw him turn to glare murderously after the departing one, and abruptly he began to curse with a freedom, fluency, and point that would have drawn admiration from any veteran muleskinner.

The burden of his tirade ran to the effect that Jim Haskins considered himself a little tin wonder with red-striped wheels, as a stock-buyer. Actually, this bunch of horses upon which he had stumbled blindly—the only way he ever found anything—was the sort of purchase no man with the morality of a misbegotten descendant of a coyote and a rattlesnake would touch with the end of a California lariat—a California rope being just twice the length of that used in Texas.

Ware drifted to that end of the gallery and listened with interest. When Vickery paused for breath, he ventured a soft remark concerning Haskins's opinion of Vickery, which he intimated hesitatingly had been widely published by Haskins.

"He did, did he?" snarled Vickery. "Why, the low-down polecat! I swung bigger deals than that tarant'ler ever seen, an' swung 'em left-handed, I did! There ain't nothin' worth buyin' in all this frazzled-out country today. Ever'body knows that. An' *he* tries to come it over me because he's makin' some sort o' shady deal with Bat Collyer o' the Open A. Like I says . . . nobody with any reputation could afford to deal with Bat Collyer, an' Jim Haskins is puttin' on the dog about it."

"Reckon Collyer's up to his ol' tricks?" inquired Ware blandly at a venture.

"Reckon he is," repeated Vickery contemptuously. "Reckon a polecat ever changes his smell? I'll lay my oath on a mile-high stack o' prayer books that nine out o' ten of them hundred an' fifty head Haskins is buyin' will have vented brands nobody in this country ever heard about . . . an' bills o' sale signed by more John Does than ever figgered in a Phila-delphia lawsuit."

"Where's Haskins loadin' 'em?" snapped Ware, forgetting diplomatic methods for the moment.

"Picacho Station, o' course," said Vickery, then he looked suspiciously at Ware. "How come you never knowed that, if you know Collyer and Haskins?"

"All I know about 'em's what I heard around today," shrugged Ware. "The way Haskins was talking, I kind of got interested in the deal."

He left the disgruntled Vickery shortly, fading out of the picture in an unobtrusive way for which he had a certain reputation in the rangers. As he went by back ways toward the corral behind the sheriff's office, it occurred to him that this might well prove a wild-goose chase, this galloping down to Picacho Station to look at a bunch of Open A horses.

Just because this Collyer's got a bad name's no sign he got hold of Rocket, he told himself gloomily. *He might have all the good intentions in the world to whirl the long rope over a good horse's head and just never get the chance.*

But it was the nearest thing to a clue he had stumbled upon, the first indication he had found that any horses were being disposed of. So he got the deputy's roan saddled and led him quietly out of the corral, having no desire to see either Robey or the big-mouthed Thomason.

Picacho Station was but a small frame building serving the railroad's agent, a water tank, some loading pens, and a couple of adobe houses. There were three or four cotton-woods near the pen; otherwise it was typically a desert station.

Ware came quietly up to the station house and dismounted. The lathered roan would tell how hard he had been ridden for twenty sultry miles, so Ware left him on the blank side of the house and drifted around to where dust and noise were apparent in the pens and about the cars on the siding. He knew that little, if any, loading had been done for, as he came, he had seen the plume of smoke from the engine that had brought those cars leaving Picacho.

There were voices quite plain in the station house, one conciliatory, youthful, the other a fierce rumble. Ware gave little heed to these. He went on down to the pens, and in his eyes was the beginning of a greenish war flame.

The buyer, Jim Haskins, was at the pens, watching two 'punchers who were rigging a gangway into a car. Ware approached unobserved and stepped upon a slat of the nearest pen to look for Rocket. Carefully he studied the animals through the dust they were kicking up, but he saw nothing of that fine, lean black head and long mane. So he made the best of the situation and moved over to Haskins.

"Howdy," he said, and the buyer whirled upon him to stare hard. "Nice-looking bunch of horses you're shipping. Selling any here?"

"Nary one," said Haskins curtly. "Belong to Bingham Brothers, an' I'm shippin' to 'em. If yuh want anything yuh see here, yuh'll have to follow the train an' buy from the big bosses. I buy. I don't sell."

"Of course," Ware nodded. "I don't know just what you got here, so I don't know as I'd be interested enough to chase your train. But they do say about me that there's a certain kind of animal I'd follow clean across the United States."

Haskins eyed him curiously, entirely without friendliness. "An' what kind o' beast might that partic'lar one be?" he inquired.

"Well, it might be a chestnut stallion."

"Then yuh wouldn't be interested in this bunch a-tall," grunted Haskins flatly. "No such thing here."

"I said it *might* be," Ware grinned mirthlessly. "Really, it's a seventeen-hand black stallion without a brand showing, six-year-old come September."

Haskins's face was blank, nor did the hands upon his hips twitch that Ware could see. He merely shrugged, as if the subject held no interest for him. Then Ware whistled suddenly, a long, shrill note that penetrated the stamping of the horses in the pens, the muffled, profane comments of the sweating 'punchers. In the pens pandemonium broke loose. Horses kicked and squealed and plunged.

The rails of those pens were built big enough to keep in the best of jumpers, or so the builders had thought, but Rocket, given room for run and take-off, might have surprised the pen makers. Confined, as he was, there was no such room, but Ware was running down to the gate, heedless of Haskell's angry yell. He threw open the gate and to him, shouldering horses to right and left, came Rocket in answer to a second whistle. Ware let him out, then slammed the gate again.

"What the hell d' yuh think yuh're doin'?" came a snarl from behind him.

Slowly, deliberately, keeping his hands at his sides, Ware turned. Haskins was covering him with steady gun muzzle.

"Mister," drawled Ware, "this here's my stallion, Rocket. Stolen from me yesterday. No trouble to prove ownership, either. He'll do anything I tell him to do and . . . he's branded Flying W."

"He ain't branded a-tall," snarled Haskins. "An' I wouldn't give a li'l bitty damn if he was to be covered with brands. I bought him. He belongs to my firm. He's goin' to be shipped with the rest o' my bunch."

"Underside the tail, he's branded," Ware said, as if not hearing the buyer's remarks. "Flying W. And you saw him come to my whistle. He'll play dead and get up, as I tell him. Now, I hate to see a man cheated, but this here's my stallion, and I'm Ware, Texas Ranger. Put down your gun, fella!"

"I said he's stayin' here! I. . . ."

Ware stepped suddenly sideways—away from Rocket—and Haskins's bullet sang between them to strike a post of the loading pens. The new guns Ware had never tried out, and this factor was the buyer's salvation, for it was no time to pick and choose the spot at which one aimed. Ware pulled with speed like that of a snake sliding into a hole; he fired with intent to remove Haskins from the scene. But the gun carried to the left, and the buyer dropped with a smashed shoulder. Ware kicked the Colt aside and bent to search his victim. No other weapons.

A shot came from a corner of the pen. Ware whirled as he heard the bullet go singing away across the open. After Ware's shots, a 'puncher from the car came staggering into sight, fell flat, then sat up to nurse with his right hand the bullet hole in his left upper arm. The other 'puncher was streaking it for the station house, from which ran now a short, tremendously wide man with sweeping mustaches who roared angrily as he came and carried a Colt in either hand.

"Stop!" called Ware thinly. "You're bucking the rangers, fella! Stop, else I'll have to stop you!"

For answer, the man jerked up his weapons and blazed away, right hand, left hand. Ware, standing still, fired deliberately, and down upon his face on the track the stocky man came crashing. Ware squatted, waiting. There were still two men in the station house.

"Inside there!" he called. "You better come on out . . . peaceful. Nobody's going to hurt you. I'm a Texas Ranger."

In the doorway, then, appeared a smallish, pale-faced man. Even across the forty yards intervening, Ware could see that his elevated hands were shaking.

"I'm the agent!" cried this one shrilly. "The other Open A boy will come out if he's sure you aren't going to kill him."

"Tell him to come on. I've no feud with the Open A. This

222

fella here just asked for what he got."

So the 'puncher who had run followed the station agent, and they walked slowly up to where Ware waited with guns at hips and feet apart.

"Who's this last one I drilled?" asked Ware, nodding toward the stocky man.

"That's the boss, Pat Collyer," said the 'puncher. "He saw yuh a-augurin' with Haskins, an' he 'lowed he was goin' to give yuh some manners to take across the heavenly river with yuh. Kill him?"

"Don't know. Let's look. Turn him over."

When the 'puncher had obeyed, it was obvious that Collyer's days were ending. Ware watched grimly. It was not the first time he had stood so, over a man he had dropped. By his fierce Texan code, the man who elected the arbitration of Judge Colt had no right to complain when the decision went against him. Nor did Ware's own part as executioner of the decision worry him. It had been an even break; he had stood in peril of his own life.

"Where'd you get that stallion, Collyer?" he asked, seeing the dying man's eyes open.

"Go . . . to . . . hell," Collyer snarled weakly.

"He bought him offen somebody none o' the rest o' us seen a-tall," the 'puncher volunteered. "Brought him in this mawnin' offen the range an' says he got him from a fella driftin' through that was broke. Had a swell silver-trimmed saddle, too. Haskins bought the stallion fer three-fifty. Saddle's on Bat's hoss down by the far pen now. I wouldn't tell yuh all this," he added with humorous lift of wide mouth, "only Bat's cashin' in. Usual, Open A boys don't open up a hell of a lot to the rest o' the world."

"Come on, now, Collyer," said Ware, stooping beside the gasping figure. "You're going to be wandering in a little spell.

'Twas a fair break. You know that. Come on and tell me a thing or two . . . you roped me out of the saddle, now, didn't you?"

"Nope, I never," wheezed Collyer. "I'm cashin' in . . . but . . . I got a . . . downhill drag. I could . . . tell yuh . . . heaps about the . . . robberies . . . but . . . I won't. Gimme . . . drink."

The 'puncher produced a pint flask from his chaps pocket. When he took it away from Collyer's lips, he regarded it mournfully. "My stars," he groaned. "Killin' him sure made him dry."

"Yuh think yuh're ridin' a kind o' crooked trail, don't yuh?" grinned Collyer, finding connected speech in the rotgut. "Hell. Yuh don' know nothin', yit. Time yuh ride a piece farther, yuh'll figger she's worse'n a spiderweb, that trail. An' I *could* point yuh straight. But here's where I'm evenin' up with yuh, Ranger. I . . . don't give a whoop . . . about the robber business . . . I just figger to even up. . . ."

That was the last he would say. Ware turned him over to the agent, talking to the 'puncher as he saddled Rocket. Haskins was left to take care of himself. Ware turned back to Monitor with the roan trailing. He had Rocket back and his saddle. To his white-handled guns he might have to say *adiós* for good and all, but he was light-hearted withal. He felt now like going to work on the actual mystery of these odd robberies.

He wondered how far that 'puncher's account might be trusted. He found himself prone to take him at face value; the fellow seemed a good-humored sort of petty rascal. He would swing the long rope at his boss's bidding, but, when the joke was on his side, he would admit it. He had vowed that Ware could not be right in suspecting Bat Collyer of being one of the mysterious robbers. He had said that on the Open A the crimes were discussed by all hands, and each time he, personally, had known Collyer's whereabouts at the time of a robbery. Still, Ware had the instinctive conviction that in recovering Rocket he had stumbled upon a line leading—invisibly, perhaps, but yet directly—to the robberies.

He put Rocket and the roan in the corral behind the sheriff's office, having unsaddled them. As he came in the back way and dropped the saddles on the floor, he heard the scrape of chairs in the office. He went in to face Robey and Dan Thomason.

"Saw yuh'd gone out," grinned Robey. "Find anything?"

"Maybe I'd better go get the coroner before you begin your story," Thomason said quickly, simulating respectful interest.

"Maybe you had," drawled Ware with steady stare. "Send him up to Picacho. He'll find Jim Haskins up there."

Thomason's face was a study in mixed emotions. Blank surprise, incredulity, then that mocking grin playing upon his thick lips. "So Jim Haskins is the stage robber!" he cried. "Well, now."

"No-o, I never said that. Happens he's not dead, either. Just got a hole in his shoulder. But . . . I had a little talk with Bat Collyer before he cashed in."

Robey and Thomason gaped at him. Ware was enjoying himself tremendously. His cookery of the crow had begun, he thought.

"Yuh downed Collyer! Bat Collyer!" gasped Robey. "Son, he's one o' the most previous gunfighters for a hundred miles any direction."

"Was," corrected Ware grimly. "He had my stallion and sold him to Haskins. He was riding my saddle on his own horse. I kind of suspicioned him, at first, of being one of the stage robbers. But I learned different."

"He tell you where he got hold of your horse?" Thomason was staring with new eyes at the smallish, negligent-postured figure.

"Nah. He was sore at me for downing him."

"Well, he's dead, anyhow," shrugged Thomason, grinning pleasantly. "Reckon we can spare Bat, all right." He began to whistle beneath his breath.

"Where yuh-all goin'?" asked Robey respectfully of Ware.

"Out to wander a little bit. I just thought of something."

He *had* thought of something, and he wanted to be by himself to mull it over. If this vague hunch were right—if only it were right. . . . He turned off the main street to squat in the striped shade of a corral. He brought out Durham and papers and rolled six cigarettes, which he laid carefully in a row before him. Then he put one in his mouth, lit it, and became as motionless as a Mexican—or a graven image. An hour passed; the cigarettes vanished one by one. Suddenly he straightened.

If a fella had just stuck up the stage, and was riding back toward Monitor . . . if this fella was to run into Bat Collyer and Bat was to say . . . 'So it's you that's been robbing the stage!' . . . if they were to talk, and Bat was to announce himself in on the loot and take Rocket for part of his share . . . if, then, this robber was to hear Bat Collyer'd been downed, wouldn't he be real happy? Wouldn't his being happy kind of shine all over his face?

Slowly he grinned. Then he epitomized his speculation. *If the robber, on whom Bat Collyer had the deadwood, were happy at news of Collyer's death, then did it work in reverse? Was the man who seemed so strangely happy at his news the robber?* Little things made him think, not that he was surely right, but that he could easily be right. *He hasn't got enough freighting business to keep a burro alive. But having a freighting business gives him excuses for rambling around a lot. He could ramble on the days the stage was stuck up. Question . . . who's that other gunny that was trailing along beside him? Fella that turned off the trail . . . or kept to it, if it was Dan Thomason who did the turning off?*

He went swiftly back to the corral, got Rocket saddled, and was gone without ostentation. He rode until he could find in the soft, now badly tracked-up dust of the stage road those twin rows of hoof marks that had led to the scene of the robbery. He got down to study them in a favorable spot on the edge of the road, where they had not been tracked over by other horses.

As he squatted, staring at them, something odd struck his practiced eye—their amazing similarity. He was pondering this as he swung up and rode on toward the low bank from which he had been roped. There could be a such a thing as twins among horses, he supposed, but certainly it was not usual.

It was not hard to discover the spot where the stage robbers had lain in wait. This was not the bank top itself, but a shallow arroyo behind the bank. It was floored for the most part by a broad reef of limestone rock on which no prints would show, but something twinkled here in the afternoon sunlight. Mechanically, Ware bent and picked up a couple of tiny, crumpled bits of metal. They did not identify themselves. He shook his head, dropped them finally in a pocket, and squatted over a patch of black adobe soil in which the hoof prints he had been studying showed in an almost plaster cast.

I think I'd kind of like to take one of these prints back to town and then snoop around friend Thomason's corral a little bit, he mused grimly. *Might just find their mates there.*

He tried it experimentally. It was not hard to cut out a square of the sticky earth and wrap it in a slicker so that it could be carried without damage. So he came back to Monitor with the bundle before him on the saddle. He went to Thomason's adobe and called softly. No answer. Probably the freighter was still with Robey; he seemed to spend most of his time in the sheriff's office. Ware rode on around to the corral and began to hunt. At last he found a print that looked similar to that upon the earth in the slicker.

He got his specimen out and laid it beside the suspicious track. No doubt of their kinship! And in a closed box stall he found a tall bay horse whose hoofs made tracks matching both the prints outside—that on the ground and that on Ware's sample cast. He hesitated a moment, then slipped inside Thomason's house. It had a couple of rooms, one used for bedroom, the other for kitchen. Ware poked about and found in a closet beneath dusty odds and ends his sombrero, his boots, his *charro* jacket, and his twin white-handled Colts. With grim lip-tightening, he replaced the clothing borrowed from the deputy with his own, setting on his sombrero, pulling on his own boots, reholstering his own Colts. But voices in the yard interrupted him. He stole to the door, carrying his jacket over an arm.

Robey and Thomason stood in the yard, staring at Rocket. Ware was outside and almost upon them before they heard his feet. He was grinning a little.

"Hunting for you-all," he greeted them cheerfully. "Wanted to tell you about finding the rest of my stuff."

He had to give credit to the devil. Thomason's face wore a good counterfeit of no more than the most innocent of interest. Robey scowled uncertainly at the ranger.

"Found them horse trails same as you did every time," Ware went on quickly, addressing Robey. "Brought back a sample print in a piece of dirt. Scouted around corrals to see if I could match it. And I did! The robber's horse . . . one robber's horse, that is . . . is right yonder in that stall. The big bay. Whose horse is that, Thomason?"

"Bay? Big bay? Why, the only horse there is mine," frowned Thomason. "It couldn't have been used by a robber . . . so far as I know."

"Was, though," grinned Ware sardonically. "Let's check the prints, Sheriff. Want you to be sure as I am."

So they brought out the bay and compared his hoof prints with that on Ware's adobe earth.

The sheriff nodded slowly. "Right! But . . . how . . . how come there was never no prints leadin' back to town? Thomason's hoss, but he never kept him long! This hoss has been in town ever' night on the day the stage was stuck up. Yuh see, Dan"—half apologetically he turned to his friend— "I checked up on ever' hoss in town I could check up on. So I know that, if this hoss was used, he had to be brought right back to town."

Ware's eyes were upon the bay's hoofs. He noticed something peculiar about the nails on the shoes. He bent to see, and from the pockets of his own jacket, upon his left arm, came a set of horseshoes. And he knew! He remembered the similarity in the prints of the *two* horses. He remembered the crumpled tips of metal—the clinchers from horseshoe nails, those were—in his pocket. Remembered, too, something that should have made its impression upon him at the moment, but had not—the fact that one set of prints showed deepest at the toe, the other at the caulk.

"You said that mining fella died, didn't you?" he grunted to Robey, and the sheriff nodded. "Yeah. Makes the robber more'n just a robber. He's wanted for murder now. This robber-murderer, he'd ride Thomason's horse out of town, and he'd change shoes on him . . . put on another set that pointed backward. After the robbery, he'd ride back to Monitor, leavin' tracks pointing out, of course. Then he'd change the shoes again. Simple."

He grinned straight up at Thomason, who still watched as if but an interested spectator.

"So you'll swing, Thomason. You lost your knife there, you know."

He shot the tall man through the arm with the Colt he had been concealing beneath the *charro* jacket, then laughed as Thomason's gun dropped to the ground.

"Guilty conscience, huh? Hell, man, I never knew you had a knife, till you started to feel for it. Robey, there's a loose board in the floor of the closet in his bedroom. He had all the rest of the stuff in there, so I reckon maybe you'll find some interesting exhibits underneath that floor. Right, huh, Thomason?"

The sheriff had been gaping incredulously from one to the other, but a glance now at the balked fury in Dan Thomason's face would have been complete assurance to a duller man, even, than the sheriff. Suddenly his face went fiery red. He half moved to the corral gate, then stopped.

"I . . . I want to git down to the post office," he said in a low voice. "I . . . there's a letter there I shore do want to git back before it goes out. I . . . I wrote askin' yo' cap'n fer another ranger an' . . . hell! We never had but *one* stage robber!"

Eugene Cunningham grew up a Texan in Dallas and Fort Worth. He enlisted in the U.S. Navy in 1914 serving in the Mexican campaign and then the Great War until his discharge in 1919. He found work as a newspaper and magazine correspondent and toured Central America. He married Mary Emilstein in 1921 and they had two daughters, Mary Carolyn and Jean, and a son, Cleve. Although Cunningham's early fiction was preoccupied with the U.S. Navy and Central America, by the mid 1920s he came to be widely loved and recognized for his authentic Western stories which were showcased in *The Frontier* and *Lariat Story Magazine*. In fact, many of the serials he wrote for *Lariat* were later expanded to book-lengths when he joined the Houghton Mifflin stable of Western writers which included such luminaries as William MacLeod Raine and Eugene Manlove Rhodes. His history of gunfighters—which he titled *Triggernometry*—has never been out of print and remains a staple book on the subject. Often his novels involve Texas Rangers as protagonists and among his most successful series of fictional adventures, yet to be collected into book form, are his tales of Ware's Kid and Bar-Nuthin' Red Ames, and ex-Ranger Shoutin' Shelley Raines. Among his most notable books are *Diamond River Man*, a re-telling of Billy the Kid's part in the Lincoln County War, *Red Range* (which in its Pocket Books edition sold over a million copies), and his final novel, *Riding Gun*. Western historian W.H. Hutchinson once described Cunningham as "as fine a lapidary as ever polished an action Western for the market place." At his best he wrote of a terrain in which he had grown up and in which he had lived much of his life, and it provides his fiction with a vital center that has often proven elusive to authors who tried to write Western fiction without that life experience behind them. Yet, as Joseph Henry Jackson wrote of him, "everywhere he went, he looked at life in terms of action, drama, romance, and danger. When you get a man who knows what men are like, what makes a story and how to write it, then you have the ideal writer in the Western field. Cunningham is precisely that."